When Cubans Went to War

Praise for
When Cubans Went to War

When Cubans Went to War is an illuminating narrative of an important period in Cuba's history, the decade that preceded the island's ten-year war of independence from Spain. The story focuses on the three children of a wealthy Havana family that, in the late 1850s, moves to a remote corner of Cuba to run a newly-acquired sugar mill. The children's lives center at first on the mill, but they then seek to move away from home and pursue their independent destinies. The Cuban-born author, Matias Travieso-Diaz, combines his literary skills and his deep knowledge of Cuba's history and its social mores to paint a fascinating picture of a society struggling to achieve a new character, free from the burdens of colonial rule.

Paul A. Gaukler

In When Cubans Went to War, the Civil War battles in the United States presage the start of similar battles in Cuba as the island begins to seek independence from Spain. These battles — over slavery, gender roles, and class attitudes — are reflected in the wealthy Serrano family. After the family moves from cosmopolitan Havana to a backwater to bet its fortune on the burgeoning sugar trade, they increasingly interact with slaves, peasants, and others marginalized by Cuba's colonial society. The growing Serrano children, curious and independent, become marginalized themselves as they explore their own identities and seek their own independence. Graciela, the eldest, explores freedom from traditional gender roles and escapes to New York to pursue forbidden love. Carmela, the middle child, explores sexual freedom with different men. Alberto, the youngest, explores Cuba's yearning for freedom from the yoke of colonial rule. The author, Matias Travieso-Diaz, is originally from Cuba and applies his deep knowledge of history, Cuba, and the arts, combined with his sharp black pen, to make When Cubans Went to War a fascinating and fast-moving story.

Alex Ferrate

Also by Matias Travieso Diaz

Cuban Transplant: An Immigrant's Recollections of Life, Love, and Loss in America, 2025. (autobiography)

The Satchel and Other Terrors – Stories of Dark Imaginings, 2023. (short story anthology)

The Potion and Other Perilous Libations – Further Stories of Dark Imaginings, 2024. (short story anthology)

Mjölnir, Gungnir & Gjallarhorn: Six heroic tales from the Norse mythology, 2024. (short story anthology)

The Dragon's Bite and Other Flights of Fantasy, 2025. (short story anthology)

Numerous Other Publications, 1997 – 2025. See, https://www.amazon.com/stores/author/B08L8QMT27/all-books?ingress=0&visitId=ce0b8459-ab2f-4652-961c-814269215783&ref_=ap_rdr

The Taíno Women, 2022. (novel) (unpublished)

The Travels of Lázaro Serrano, 2023. (novel) (unpublished)

When Cubans Went to War

Matias Travieso-Diaz

Boston, MA

This is a work of fiction. Unless otherwise indicated, all the names, characters, businesses, places, events and incidents in this book are either the product of the author's imagination or used in a fictitious manner. Any resemblance to actual persons, living or dead, actual places, or actual events is purely coincidental.

Part 1

1859

The Calm Before the Storm

Prologue

La Habana, September 1, 1851

*Those who make peaceful revolution impossible
will make violent revolution inevitable.*
John F. Kennedy

Alberto Serrano was only six years old when his uncle Leonardo took him to witness the execution of Narciso López. Along with thousands of other spectators, they gathered outside the ancient fortress known as Castillo de La Punta and watched as Spanish guards escorted López to a specially constructed dais, forced him to sit on a metal chair, shackled him down, and placed an iron collar around his neck. To the boy's horror, the executioner interrupted the prisoner's final words by rotating a bar behind the chair, advancing a screw that tightened the collar, until it strangled López to death. Alberto would forever remember how the prisoner shook violently as he tried to free himself from his bonds while his face turned purple and finally expanded grotesquely. His tongue stuck out as he asphyxiated while the crowd (for the most part) cheered in approval.

Alberto's mother Cecilia had strenuously opposed her brother-in-law's decision to take Alberto to watch the execution, arguing that a child of tender years should not be subjected to such a vicious spectacle, but Alberto's uncle insisted: "It is good that he understands from a very early age that Spain has enemies that must be strongly dealt with. Traitors like López and his crew must be destroyed. Cuba is, and will forever remain, one with the motherland, and any attempts to make us follow the shameful example of the Mexicans and the Colombians will be nipped in the bud."

Cecilia, widowed and depending on the charity of her family, swallowed her concern and yielded to her brother-in-law's demands. Alberto was the youngest and only boy of the three underage children she had been forced to raise alone upon the sudden death from yellow fever of Lázaro, her husband. Taking the child in her arms, she whispered on his ear: "Albertico, you must be strong. You are the only man in our family, so your sisters and I depend on you to do whatever needs to be done to protect us. For now, you must pay attention to your uncle, and always do as he asks. It will be better for all of us."

Alberto could not understand why the execution's victim, a middle-aged White man whose appearance was hardly threatening, deserved such cruel treatment. All the boy was told was that López had led an armed group that came from outside Cuba, landed on a beach west of La Habana, and tried to do something against the government.

Later in life, Alberto would learn that many Cubans wanted independence from Spain, complaining of economic inequality, lingering slavery, and the despotic rule of the governors Spain appointed to rule its last colony in the Americas. Others, particularly the island's White landholders, feared that a revolt would result in a slave uprising (like had happened in Haiti half a century before) or, at a minimum, bring about the abolition of slavery with adverse impacts on their interests. Further complicating matters was the notion, which López and his supporters shared but others did not, that Cuba should become part of the United States instead of an independent nation. Politicians and others in the slave-owning South of the U.S. were in favor of annexing Cuba and supported López, causing his invasion to become entangled with internal American politics.

But as he watched the gruesome execution, Alberto was oblivious of all of that. He only felt, deep in his soul, that whatever had happened that September morning was wrong and upsetting, and he wanted no part of it, and perhaps someday he would do something to prevent it from happening again.

Chapter 1

La Habana, June 1856: Graciela's Debutante Party

*I wasn't brought up as a society girl to go to balls and be a debutante
and marry the social set and money and go to parties.
… I always wanted a career.*
Lauren Bacall

*T*he formal party her mother insisted on throwing for her to
mark her fifteenth birthday was the greatest imposition Graciela
had experienced in her short life. But she understood why
her mother and uncle Leonardo wanted to organize such an
ostentatious show. For her mother, who grew in poverty and did
not have such a celebration, it was a chance to vicariously affirm
her life's eventual successes; for Leonardo, who had decided to
marry his business instead of a wife, it was the opportunity to
display his wealth and achievements before his business contacts
and the upper level of the Habana society.

In addition, los quince, the debutante ball, was a critical
point in the life of a woman. It signified that the honored girl,
the quinceañera, was ready to fulfill her public role in society;
to marry, bear children, and provide comfort and support to her
husband; and manage their household in a proper and dignified
manner. The problem was that Graciela did not feel ready to do

any of these things and doubted she would ever want to do them.

She hated housework and was not very good at it. Besides, their household slave María Dolores (who everyone called "Yaya") took care of all the cleaning and could cook and bake better than anyone else. As for finding a man and having and raising children, she was not interested. She might have to do these things someday, but for the moment her attention lay elsewhere.

Graciela wanted to write. Novels. Stories. But mainly poems. She knew by heart many works by classic Cuban bards such as Zequeira and Rubalcava, but her favorites were the new wave of poets led by José María Heredia and Gabriel de la Concepción Valdés, better known as Plácido. Heredia and Plácido attracted her by the formal freedom and the emotional content of their works, and also by the very romantic nature of their lives: both poets had embraced the cause of Cuba's independence, had died young, and had paid with their lives for their ideals. Heredia died in exile, Plácido before a firing squad.

Graciela knew she had to be careful not to be too outspoken in praising these revolutionary poets, for her uncle Leonardo was a strong supporter of the Spanish colonial administration and would have looked askance at any political dissent, expressed or implicit, from within his family. Her sister Carmela, three years younger, was just entering puberty and discovering boys and had no use for politics or the arts. That left only Albertico to serve as a potential confidant. She loved her little brother, but he was too young to be reliable, so her conversations with him had to be guarded for fear he would inadvertently give her oddness away.

Her mother was also no help. Coming from a poor family, she could barely read and write and had no interest in things outside her domestic world. Right now, her main concern was to properly introduce her oldest daughter to the upper-class society in which they moved thanks to Leonardo's wealth and connections. The coming out party, therefore, had to be a success.

***

It took months of arduous preparations to bring about Graciela's party; it was an enterprise in which the entire family collaborated. Except for her.

On a humid Saturday evening in late June, Graciela sat in an open horse-drawn carriage bedecked with garlands of flowers that cruised leisurely along the Malecón, La Habana's seaside promenade. As she waved to the spectators, the livered driver repeatedly honked a horn to draw everyone's attention to the momentous occasion.

When she arrived at the hall where the ball was to be held, Graciela was greeted by Leonardo, who escorted her through an arched entryway and along a red velvet carpet to the large reception room. There, she was met by her mother, pale as a ghost and breathing heavily from anxiety. As protocol required, Graciela bowed to her mother and thanked her for making this beautiful dream come true. Hand in hand, they strolled through the room, greeting the numerous guests who, for the first time, could admire the transformation of a plain girl into a young princess. Graciela, carefully made up and wearing a wide, snow-white dress and elbow-length gloves, had a tiara circling her carefully coiffed hair and a necklace of fake diamonds with matching dangling earrings.

The stroll concluded and Cecilia retreated to the edge of the room; the dance then began. The first dance, with music provided by a band positioned in an adjoining room, was a danza in the style of the eighteenth-century formal dances of the courts in Europe. Leonardo led his niece partly through the piece and then surrendered her to Albertico, who was only eleven but was serving as his older sister's galán. He, and fourteen other invited boys, wore formal black pants and vests, white linen shirts, and cravats.

Following the first dance, fourteen boys and an equal number of girls joined Graciela and Albertico to form a circle to perform a contradanza, another traditional dance in whose steps they had been instructed by a choreographer hired for the occasion and rehearsed for weeks before the event. The boys were dressed in the same manner as Albertico while the girls wore puffy, pastel-colored gowns in the same style as that of the quinceañera. Together, the fourteen couples constituted a miniature court gathered to render homage to Graciela and Albertico.

Dancing was then opened to the entire congregation and proceeded through a number of dances, mostly African-inspired. After a while, at a signal from Leonardo, the music stopped and the dance floor was cleared to allow the wheeling in of a huge multi-tiered cake decorated with candles and featuring figurines of Graciela's court crowned by a small doll representing her, alone at the top tier. There was a collective murmur of admiration accompanied by the entrance of serving slaves who distributed flutes filled with chilled hard cider. Once everyone had a glass at hand, Leonardo toasted: "Let us drink to my beautiful niece Graciela on her special day. May she live up to her name and grace us for many, many years to come." He and the rest of the attendees raised their flutes up in the air and drank. The toast was followed by the serving of canapés, the cutting and distributing of the cake, and more eating, drinking and dancing until the early morning hours.

***

Much later the following morning, the family met for breakfast to celebrate the event's success. They took turns praising Graciela for her beauty and poise and thanking Leonardo for his generosity in footing the staggering bill. Cecilia commented: "Graciela, it was good of you to suffer through the heat and discomfort of a full night of partying. I am sorry you had to change clothes five times throughout the evening and refresh your makeup on account of the heat."

Graciela waved dismissively and replied, smiling: "Don't worry, mother. It was all worthwhile," while at the same time thinking: "*Those were the only moments I could spend time with my dear Alicia. Thanks heaven for the heat.*"

As the last cups of coffee were served, Leonardo rose, and

8

in the same formal tone he had used the night before to toast, announced: "I have great news. Yesterday, I closed on the purchase of an estate not far from Manzanillo. It includes a small ingenio (sugar mill) on the premises, which I intend to modernize and turn into Cuba's most modern mill. I am having the manor house refurbished. It will be ready for occupation before the hurricane season starts in September." He paused to stare at his family. "We are moving to Oriente."

Cecilia was quick to protest: "What are we going to do there? My children have an education to pursue, friends, a life in La Habana."

"I need you all to come with me to help set up our new estate, which I cannot do alone. After a few months, maybe a year, you can come back to La Habana if you wish. You know, I have no other family, and I intend to leave all I own to you and your children. Thus, it is in your interest that this venture succeed, for it will make us quite wealthy. Think of it as an extended vacation in the country." He pounded on the table energetically to underscore his words.

Cecilia was unconvinced but could not oppose her brother-in-law's imperious request. "A few months in the country" might not be that bad, after all.

Chapter 2

Pilón, Oriente, March – May, 1859: Carmela's Quince

*There's nothing worse than the sequel
that's a letdown from the first movie.*
Paul Feig

*M*uch had changed in the three years since Graciela's debutante ball. Their move to the estate in Oriente had caused acrimony within the family. Cecilia and her children had resisted the move and attempted to stay behind, but Leonardo was inflexible: as head of the family after his older brother's untimely passing, he insisted that they all stay together and live in safety and comfort under the same roof, at least for a while.

By the time Cecilia's middle child, Carmela, approached the magic age of fifteen, the family was comfortably settled in the casa de vivienda (manor house) of *Santa Cruz*, a large estate that included the sugar mill. The property was located astride Pilón, a small town in southwestern Oriente province. Pilón lay near a beautiful stretch of coast but was twenty leagues from the nearest city of any size, Manzanillo—too far to reach in a day over a steep mountain road. Santiago de Cuba was 40 leagues away, a several days ride. The distances made opportunities for social interaction with the higher levels of colonial society quite limited.

Cecilia's children were affected by the isolation in various ways. Graciela missed the company of girls her age but shifted her attention to her favorite activities: reading, writing simple poems, and playing the late-model upright piano Leonardo had purchased at great cost to placate his nieces. She hardly noticed the passage of time, at least for the first few years of what she referred to as "our exile in the dark provinces."

Alberto, the most athletic member of the family, went on frequent explorations of the mountains that surrounded Pilón and was soon an expert on the flora of the virgin forests as well as the hollows, caves, and other hiding places that allowed him to escape his mother's vigilant eye. He was not above making friends with the village youngsters and often engaged in street games of football with other kids his age and older.

It was a motley crowd that gathered for those games. The children of the small village reflected the composition of the local population—a mixture of Spaniards, Black Jamaicans, escaped French colonists from Haiti, White criollos, and descendants of the native Taínos. Alberto, whose amber coloring, slanted eyes, and facial features betrayed his mixed-race heritage, fitted well with the locals and never gave a minute's thought to the race or national origin of his playmates.

Carmela was the one child who was most adversely affected by the move to Pilón. Gregarious by nature, she had left behind a warm circle of friends in La Habana and had great difficulty finding replacements in the small provincial town where she had been forced to live. She found the local teenagers barely educated and quite ignorant of the latest fashions, songs, and dances. For that reason, she limited her infrequent social interactions to a handful of boys and girls, mainly children of mill employees who at least came from good families, even if they were beneath her social standing.

Right after the Easter observances, Cecilia realized she had to do something about Carmela's fast approaching fifteenth birthday. Since everything that cost money depended on Leonardo's approval, the widow reluctantly approached her brother-in-law, who was, as always, busy buying new equipment for the mill and managing the operations of the estate. Their conversation was characteristically brief:

[Cecilia]: "Leonardo, we need to have a party for Carmela. She will turn fifteen in May."

[Leonardo]: "Of course. What did you have in mind?"

[Cecilia]: "It's a problem, because we can't go back to La Habana, and everything we will need for a decent party we can't get around here."

[Leonardo]: "Can you get it in Santiago?"

[Cecilia]: "I suppose, but we would need to seek out vendors and artists, and I don't know anybody there."

[Leonardo]: "Why don't you and Carmela make a shopping trip to Santiago and get what you need? Ruperto can drive you there on our carriage and you can take Yaya along with you. I will write Banco del Comercio to authorize you to withdraw any amounts you need."

[Cecilia]: "Is there any faster way to get to Santiago than by carriage?"

[Leonardo]: "Sorry, sister. They are starting to build a railway out of Santiago, but it will be years before it comes this way."

[Cecilia (sighing)]: "Is there a limit on the money I can draw?"

[Leonardo]: "Only the balance on my account. But I don't see how you could spend that much."

[Cecilia]: "Thank you. I will be prudent."

[Leonardo]: "Don't worry. Just keep track of how much you draw. Have a nice trip."

***

Cecilia, Carmela, and Yaya were gone for three weeks, including over seven days on the road. It was an exhausting and disappointing trip: Santiago, for all its three and a half centuries of existence, was a provincial town lacking the sophistication of La Habana. It took a lot of effort to make arrangements for what was needed for that special May 29 Sunday, but at the end (after some compromising) they had hired musicians who could play the required dances, caterers to bring and prepare food and a special birthday cake, an expatriate French dressmaker to come to Pilón to fit and create dresses for the girls and suits for the boys who would be accompanying Carmela as her attendants, and a dancing instructor to teach the children new dances, including waltzes.

Now came the hardest part: finding at least half a dozen teenage boys and girls who would be suitable for the occasion. Carmela was privately instructed, but had prevailed on her mother to let her join the local sewing club of which Cecilia was a member and was on reasonably good terms with several girls her age or older, so she was able to find six young women who were willing–indeed, honored–to become participants in the festivities. The boys, however, were a problem: Carmela knew none, and Alberto's football friends were deemed unsuitable by Cecilia, who thought of the lot as mataperros, that is, hooligans. Leonardo had to come to the rescue: he mentioned to his employees and local business associates that he needed to find half a dozen young men of good character to help celebrate his niece's coming of age. He personally interviewed the candidates that were referred to him and selected ten of them, who were then scrutinized by Cecilia, who narrowed the group to half a dozen and invited them to attend the festivities. It was a random array, representing a cross-section of the community's free families, but like other aspects of the celebration of Carmela's quince, it was the best that could be achieved under the circumstances.

As the red-letter day approached, Cecilia was heard to repeat that she and Leonardo were doing their best to duplicate, within the limits of what was possible, the success of the party they had given to Graciela years earlier. Carmela would invariably respond by telling her mother not to worry, she appreciated their efforts but having a grandiose party was not that important to her. And as matters moved along, the excitement grew, not only within the Serrano household but throughout the sleepy village that had never experienced an event of such magnitude.

Alberto was to play the same role for Carmela as he had for their older sister at Graciela's party: he was to be the birthday girl's galán. He would escort Carmela and dance with her a couple of times, but otherwise was not expected to do much entertaining. By now, however, Alberto was fourteen and was beginning to notice girls. So he was looking forward to mingling with members of the fair sex. He discussed his plans with some of his football playmates and extended a broadly worded invitation for them to crash the party:

"I don't think my mom or Uncle Leonardo would do anything to kick you out. Just make sure you wear decent clothes and don't do anything foolish." Most of his friends showed no interest in the party, but a couple of mulatto brothers, Rino and Rodolfito, indicated that they might show up to taste the lechón (roast pork), sample the birthday cake, and drink a glass of wine. "By all means, do come" replied Alberto expansively.

***

As anyone could have predicted, Carmela's party was nowhere near the grandiose event that had been staged for Graciela. There was no carriage ride along Pilón's minuscule waterfront; the lobby of the town's city hall was not designed for large gatherings and could not accommodate more than a couple of dozen occupants; and the town's folks were not sophisticated in the way most residents of La Habana were, so they felt uncomfortable wearing formal dress or doing the modern dance steps. Nonetheless, the invitees were on their best behavior and tried to do what was expected of them.

Not all those present behaved as they should. Rino and Rodolfito made good on their promise to crash the party and found themselves standing in the back of the lobby, filching tidbits off the platters as hors d'oeuvres were brought out for the guests. Even they, however, held their breaths expectantly as Carmela was led into the room by her brother.

Carmela was not ugly, but her features were ordinary, and she would not have been cataloged as a beauty. However, for the occasion of her debutante party she had been carefully made up with a thin layer of white powder that lightened her swarthy complexion. Her hair was parted with a ringlet of curls dripping over one shoulder; strands of fragrant jasmine blooms hung from both sides of her head. She was dressed in an off-white full length silk dress with matching laces and flowers and long white silk evening gloves with lace trimmings. Her face was enhanced with darkened lashes and eyebrows, soft rouge on her cheeks, and light pink lip stain. She was wearing gold earrings, a white lace choker from which dangled a dozen seed pearls, and a gold chain holding a starburst gold pendant nesting alternating tiny diamonds and seed pearls. She was a sight that had never been seen in that village, and her entrance elicited an admiring gasp from everyone.

Alberto led his sister in a circuit around the lobby and the two came to stop in the center of the room, at which point a signal was given to the orchestra stationed in a room behind the lobby, and the couple started twirling to the strands of Joseph Lanner's *Die Krönungswalzer*. Brother and sister were experienced dancers, having been trained for two quinceañera parties, but this waltz was a newly learned skill, and they encountered a few stumbling moments, partly due to the unsuitability of the satin evening shoes Carmela was wearing. Nonetheless, they managed to finish the dance and were rewarded by a warm round of applause by the attendees.

At that point a guide, the bastonero, organized the order and position of the couples that took to the floor and led them in a series of dances, mainly contradanzas and habaneras, forming them in lines, circles, quartets, trios, and duets. The dances became more and more animated, helped perhaps by the saoco (rum and coconut milk) cocktails that were continuously being distributed to both the couples on the floor and the spectators.

Rino and Rodolfito had remained out of sight most of the evening but, as alcohol began coursing through their veins, they became less inhibited and joined the dancers in an habanera and stayed on the floor thereafter. There were murmurs of disapproval and Cecilia pursed her lips, trying to decide whether to intervene and disrupt the proceedings. She hesitated and let matters go on.

The next number played by the orchestra was a danza, *El Sungambelo*, which was well-known throughout Cuba. It was a favorite of Carmela and Alberto, who had danced it together many times. As they were starting to dance, Rodolfito walked over, tapped Alberto on the shoulder, and offered his arm to the surprised Carmela.

The danza had a particular feature: the male held his female partner in a closed dance position, later adopted by the waltz. This holding position between the partners allowed a greater degree of intimacy than was afforded by dances in which the partners did not touch. Thus, Rodolfito's move was quite daring. Alberto grimaced and stepped aside, leaving Rodolfito and Carmela moving to the slow, sensuous rhythm of the music.

"You are the most excellent woman I ever laid eyes on!" whispered Rodolfito, his voice a bit slurred by alcohol.

"You are drunk … and you stink!" replied Carmela, teetering between indignation and amusement.

"My dear, what you smell is bay rum cologne, I spent half my salary on a bottle hoping to meet some beauty, and by Saint Anne I did!" he replied, squeezing her shoulder.

"You are lying" she replied, suppressing a smile. "You just have been drinking my uncle's saoco."

"I may have had a sip or two, but if I am drunk, it is because the sight of you has made me lose my senses."

As they continued to gyrate, other couples moved back so that, in a few moments, they were alone in the center of the room. "Let go of me! Everyone is watching us!" protested Carmela.

"I'll never let you go. I…" started Rodolfito before he was yanked away from the girl by a extremely upset Leonardo. "Get your hands of my niece, you filthy bum!" he shouted, seizing Rodolfito by the neck and starting to drag him towards the front door.

"Hey, don't touch my brother!" screamed Rino, who had been watching the proceedings with amusement that turned to alarm. Rino tried to free Rodolfito from Leonardo's grasp, who turned around and punched Rino hard on the face, dropping him to the floor.

Pandemonium erupted. Several people moved to restrain Leonardo, who had released Rodolfito and hovered above Rino, who was sitting on the ground nursing a broken nose. Leonardo pointed the finger at Rino and ordered: "Both of you, get out of here right now before I call the alguacil and have you thrown in jail!"

Rino got to his feet sullenly and headed for the door, murder in his eyes. He was joined by Rodolfito, who in the meantime had pleaded with Carmela in a low voice: "Can I please see you again? Please! Please!?"

Startled, Carmela moved her head up and down once.

Chapter 3

Pilón, June, 1859: Aftermath

Some events had come to their dire conclusions, for out of present tragedy so often rose future triumph; the result of sorrowful recriminations was often the catalyst of progress.
Anne McCaffrey, To Ride Pegasus

*C*ecilia had never seen her brother-in-law so angry. She knew Leonardo had a temper, but most of the time he kept it under control. Obviously, he was upset that Carmela's party, on which he had invested a lot of money, had been ruined by the incident with those ruffians, and his reputation as an amiable businessman had been impaired.

When the last remaining guests had departed, Leonardo got the family together in the empty city hall and vented his frustration. "How did those negros sucios get the notion that they could get away with crashing our party?" He let out an angry sigh. "It was my fault, I guess, for not posting a couple of guys at the door to make sure that only our guests could come in…"

Alberto kept his eyes lowered, debating whether to fess up or reveal his part in the fiasco. He decided he had to come clean for

Carmela's sake. "Er… I know those guys from playing football around town…" He paused for a second to gather his courage: "I may have told them it would be fine for them to show up and have some cake…"

"You, imbecile!" exploded Leonardo. "I should take it off your hide!" He started in the boy's direction, but Cecilia moved between them. "What is done is done. Nobody could have predicted what happened." She put her arm protectively around her son.

"Anyway, it was a very nice party, and I enjoyed myself a lot" cut in Carmela.

Later, Carmela questioned her brother: "Who were those fellows you invited to my party?"

"I dunno, I play football with them and other guys on weekends on the lot behind the church."

"You invited them, and you don't know anything about them?"

"Well, I know that Rodolfito, the one who danced with you, is an apprentice at Galván's blacksmith shop. I don't think his brother Rino works anywhere."

"Where do they live?"

"In a shack at the edge of town. They are very poor."

"Also quite brazen. Where did that Rodolfito get the notion that I would want to have anything with him?"

Graciela, who was overhearing the conversation, cut in: "Maybe he has read *Romeo y Julieta*."

"I don't think so. I am pretty sure he and his brother have no schooling, though the parish priest taught them to read and write" replied Alberto. "Anyhow, he was surely acting out of character being so forward with Carmela. He is usually quiet and well-behaved. Not at all like Rino."

"He was probably blinded by my beauty" chuckled Carmela.

"Alcohol makes us do the weirdest things" replied Graciela, not trying to hide a smile.

Chapter 4

Pilón, June, 1859: Getting to the Church on Time

I got to get there in the morning
Spruced up and lookin' in my prime.
Alan Jay Lerner, My Fair Lady

*R*odolfo was burning with desire to lay eyes again on the beautiful Carmela Serrano. The girl had silently consented to their meeting but getting it to happen was nearly impossible. Showing up at the Serrano manor house was out of the question: in the aftermath of the party Leonardo had bought a fierce mastiff whose menacing barks could be heard two blocks away and posted an armed watchman to keep undesirables from disturbing the family. Rodolfo had known that Carmela left the house to attend her sewing club meetings in the company of her mother and Yaya, but Rodolfo had no female relatives or friends who were members of the club and could serve as go-betweens.

But there was the church. The women in the Serrano household attended services at the parish church, a two-room structure located only a few blocks from the manor house. If the weather was good, the four women went on foot to the mid-morning masses on Sundays and holidays. Leonardo was too busy, he claimed, to accompany them except on special occasions, and had felt no need to send Ruperto or some other of his servants or employees to escort them.

"If I could only set Carmela aside for five minutes, I would be able to make my case and try to win her heart" lamented Rodolfo to his brother.

"And you want me to help you get some alone time with your sweetie" replied Rino, sarcasm dripping from his voice.

"I don't see how you could manage that" replied Rodolfo.

"Oh, I think I could manage that. The question is whether I want to do it."

"Oh, come on Rino, don't play with me. You know how important this is."

Rino remained silent for a few moments. "All right, I will do it for you, seeing that you are my favorite brother. When do you want to do it?"

"Next time they will go to church is Sunday morning, for the nine o'clock mass. Say some time before nine?"

"Fine. This is what we will do."

***

At twenty minutes to nine, Cecilia, her daughters, and Yaya emerged from the street that led to the parochial church, walking by a vacant lot adjacent to the church. As they did, Rodolfo – who was stationed behind the church – waved his arms widely, signaling for a gaggle of teenagers led by Rino to enter the vacant lot. The boys split into two camps and started screaming at each other. What appeared to be a vicious fight broke out and someone started overturning trash receptacles and setting them on fire.

Cecilia shouted in a quivering voice: "Let's run into the church! Quick!" She was, as usual, the leader of the group and soon entered the church with Graciela close on her heels. At that point, Rodolfo emerged from hiding, seized Carmela by the arm, and dragged her behind the building while at the same time motioning to Yaya to join them.

"Carmela, I am desperately in love with you and must see you. Please meet with me soon so we can talk, or I will kill myself!" There was utter desperation in his voice and Carmela hesitated a moment.

"You are out of your mind! But don't do anything rash! I don't want to have that on my conscience."

"I swear that I will!"

Carmela stared at the boy intently. He was a handsome, tall, strong looking youth of mixed race like her. He did not seem in any way threatening, and she felt flattered by his attention. "All right. Yaya goes to the market Monday mornings to get fresh produce for the family. I will send a note for you with her. Now let me go, before my mother comes out looking for me!"

"Thank you, my love!" replied Rodolfo, letting go and disappearing behind the church.

"That boy is crazy as a goat!" declared Yaya, rolling her eyes.

"I know, but don't tell mama what just happened!" warned Carmela.

"I won't. But you take care, you hear!" replied the slave, giving her ward a sly look.

Chapter 5

Pilón, June, 1859: Brief Encounter

Every sunset brings the promise of a new dawn.
Ralph Waldo Emerson

*T*hey met at sunset at the main Pilón dock, a concrete structure with an ironwork extension that allowed small and medium sized craft to drop anchor and bring on or unload merchandise. Deserted at this late hour, it sat totally in the open, visible from the nearby sugar mill and manor house. It held a wooden shack where port officials had their office. Carmela had secured a key to the shack and waited inside while Yaya, shivering in the evening breeze, stood guard outside.

They had to wait only a few minutes before a figure emerged from the shadows. It was Rodolfo, wearing work clothes: cotton pants, a tattered shirt, a straw hat, and a heavy leather apron. His first words were an apology for his dress: "I could not get away from the shop until just now. Galván is busy these days."

"Never mind that" replied Carmela. "What is it that you must talk to me about, Rodolfito?"

"Oh." He was a bit deflated by the girl's tart tone but recovered. "Carmela, please call me Rodolfo from now on. I have aged from thinking about you since your party. I love you!"

"How can you say you love me? We have barely met, and not under the best circumstances."

"I know. I'm sorry for my behavior and my brother's. But see, the moment you entered that room, dressed all in white like an angel from heaven, I felt like my life was changed. I want to live with you, or not at all!"

"That is ludicrous. I'm just an ordinary girl. What's there about me that you find so attractive?"

"I can't describe it. The way you move. How you carry yourself. Your smile…"

"I am no beauty. There must be many girls in this town that are better looking than I."

"I have met the other girls. None can compare with you."

"How old are you?"

"I'll be seventeen this December."

"I just turned fifteen. Don't you think you are too young to be serious about me? Won't you change your mind in a week or year?"

"I know my heart. My feelings won't change."

"Well, supposing you are right. How about me? I don't feel any attraction for you."

"I think you are mistaken. I noticed how you looked at me when we were dancing. You may not love me yet, but you are at least interested."

"I sort of admired your daring, but that does not mean I feel anything for you."

"Well, at least you don't hate me for ruining your party. That is a good start."

Carmela could not help breaking into a small smile. "No, I don't *hate* you but…"

The boy did not let her finish. "Well, that's a start! I would hope we can at least be friends."

"I don't know. We are so different. I don't think we have much in common."

"Not true. We are both young, smart, and have a good heart. What else do we need to become friends?"

"You make it sound like it would be a simple matter. For one thing, my family surely would not approve of our being friends. How would we meet? Where? What would we do? You work and I study and have my own social life, and the two do not seem to be compatible."

"Those are details that can be worked out. All I ask is that you give us a chance to get to know each other better."

There was a long silence. For the first time, Carmela stared intently at Rodolfo, whose face was contorted with anxiety. He had fine features and, except for his kinky hair, could have passed for White. Overall, he was handsome and appeared honest and sincere. The social life opportunities in this backwater were not that great and returning to La Habana was not an immediate prospect. Perhaps this eager boy would prove good company, if it could be arranged without upsetting matters with the rest of the family.

"Well, I am willing to give friendship a try, but you should have absolutely no illusions of anything else. You can send me word with Yaya as to how you want to proceed. And remember, I don't want to get in trouble with my relatives."

Chapter 6

Pilón, June, 1859: Meeting at the Market

> *Thou wast the prettiest babe that e'er I nursed*
> *An I might live to see thee married once.*
> Nurse, Romeo and Juliet, Act IV, Scene 3

Yaya, **usually quite** placid, became agitated and began gesticulating angrily. "Are you out of your mind? Take the missy to that bar, *El Malecón*? To hang out with the criminals and the drunks and the putas? Not on your life!"

Rino tried to calm the slave, whose explosion had caused heads to turn all around them in the market. "No, señora, it's not like that. Me and my bro wouldn't dream of having your pretty miss mingle with the riff-raff. Listen, we have it all figured out."

It took a while before the slave's volcanic eruption abated to the point Rino could go on with his explanation. "See, me and Rodolfito are friends with Luciano, the owner of the bar and have cut a deal with him."

"A deal?" asked the Black woman suspiciously.

"Yeah. See, you will bring Carmelita through the back entrance and walk a few steps until you hit the bar's back room, where Luciano stores the liquor. I will have a table and chairs set up there. Your miss and my brother will sit in complete privacy, and none'll know they are there."

"I don't like it" insisted Yaya. "If Carmelita is seen there with your brother, her reputation will be ruined. And for what?" Her voice was rising again, and Rino hastened to stem the flow of angry words. "Nobody will, Yaya. I and my friends will stand guard in front and rear of the bar to block anyone from getting in."

"I'm not telling the miss about this crazy scheme of yours."

"Come on, Yaya" said Rino placatingly. "Carmelita is waiting for word from us. Let her make her own decisions. You tell her, or I will need to tell her myself."

The slave was scared by the possibility of Carmela being approached by the ruffian. "No, no. I'll tell her" she declared.

"But she will laugh at the idea. She's a very sensible girl, although a little bit impulsive at times," thought the servant.

Carmela, however, did not laugh at the proposition. It was a wild and dangerous plan, but at least it meant that Rodolfito was serious about her. She felt flattered and somewhat excited by the opportunity to do something rebellious and a little naughty that broke the dull routine of her life in Pilón.

"Next time you see either brother at the market, get exact details so we can plan for the meeting. I will do this once, and then never again."

Chapter 7

Pilón, June, 1859: In the Backroom

Many a time from a bad beginning
great friendships havesprung up.
Terence

*T*he atmosphere was tense as Rino escorted the women to the small room in the back of the bar and withdrew to stand guard by the back door. Yaya, who was accompanying her ward, sat on a stool against the wall, ready to snap in defense of Carmela if the situation warranted it. She was sweating profusely, in part from the stifling summer heat that filled the room, but mostly from nerves. Bringing the young girl to this den of perdition was the hardest chore she had ever had to perform, and she was expecting that something dreadful would happen at any moment.

Shortly after Carmela took a seat on one side of the small table, Rodolfo entered through the bar side and sat across from her. "Thank you for agreeing to meet me here. It means the world to me."

"I have thought about it and decided we cannot be friends because we move in different circles, and you and your brother already have had a bad start with our family."

"I don't think our start was all that bad. You seemed to enjoy dancing with me. But put that aside. Do you find me ugly or repulsive?"

Carmela felt she had to shake her head in denial. "No, I don't."

"Have I offended you in any way? Do I look like a criminal, or put you in fear for your safety?" Carmela uttered a silent negation.

"So, what's the harm in us sitting together having a nice conversation every now and then?"

Carmela sighed.

"Good. Let me tell you about myself. I'm not from these parts. My parents lived in a *palenque* east of here; my father was killed when the Spanish government raided their settlement eight years ago, but my mother, brother, and I escaped and came to Pilón. We were given shelter in the parish church and my mother was hired as a laundress for the church. She had a bad heart and died two years ago. Since then, Rino and I have been on our own, living in a shack the church gave to our mother. Father Pastor has looked after us from a distance and has taught us to read and write. As you know, I am an apprentice to Galván, the town's blacksmith; Rino does what odd jobs he can. We are poor but honest."

"How about your grandparents?"

"I never learned about my father's ancestors, only that he was an escaped slave. My grandmother on my mother's side came to Cuba sixty years ago when the troubles started in Haiti and her owner, along with his family and slaves, had to escape to Cuba. My father met my mother in Santiago and talked her into going to the palenque with him. How about your family?"

"My grandfather on my father's side had a very interesting life and left behind an account of his travels. He was of mixed race: Black, White, and maybe even Indian. He made a fortune from selling for a health spa resort a farm he had bought near La Habana, and married grandmother Graciela when he was in his forties. He had two boys, my father now dead and Uncle Leonardo, who became a financier and increased our property holdings. Mother is from a poor family in a small town near La

Habana, nothing special about them."

"So, we are not that different, are we?"

"I guess not," allowed Carmela.

***

Carmela had to shake Yaya awake; the slave had fallen asleep, her head resting against the wall and her mouth whistling with a soft snore. Yaya became immediately alert and gasped in alarm. "Are you safe? What did that boy do to you?" she screeched.

"Nothing, Yaya. He's a good boy" replied Carmela reassuringly.

"What time is it?" asked Yaya, rubbing sleep from her eyes.

"It's getting late. Let's go home before night falls."

"How long was I asleep?"

"At least an hour" smiled Rodolfo, getting up to stand next to the women.

"Oh, Changó bendito, I should be whipped. What happened?" she asked again, suspiciously.

"We just talked. I'll tell you on the way home. Now we must go."

The slave got to her feet slowly, wincing from the effort.

"When will I see you again?" ventured the boy, wistfully.

"I don't know. Let me figure it out. I'll send word with Yaya."

Rodolfo let out a sigh of relief. "Alright. I hope it is soon."

"Greedy boy" smiled Carmela, heading for the back door, followed by her slave.

Chapter 8

Pilón, June - July, 1859: Behind the Church

The **routine was** set quickly: Every Friday night at 8 pm a number of devout ladies would gather at the parish church to pray a novena, which in the month of June was addressed to Saint Anthony of Padua, the saint who supposedly helped find lost things or mend affairs gone off-kilter. Carmela would leave home early "to engage in her own private prayer," inviting her mother and Graciela to join her; she knew full well that neither would be interested in such devotions and would stay home.

Yaya and Carmela would arrive shortly before seven and, instead of entering the church, would proceed to a small garden to the side of the building. Carmela would sit on a bench in the garden, Yaya standing guard in front of her to provide cover and warn of possible intruders. Rodolfo would arrive at seven o'clock sharp and sit next to the girl. They would chat amiably until almost eight, and when Yaya alerted them that other women were approaching, the couple would stand. Rodolfo would kiss her hand and disappear while Carmela would enter the church and pray to Saint Anthony for help of retrieving whatever she might have lost.

In time, their conversations became more intimate, their whispered voices turned more tender, until at the end of the third weekly meeting, Rodolfo kissed Carmela on the cheek and caressed her bare arm, sending a chill down her spine. Yaya, watching the proceedings with mounting concern, grabbed her mistress and whisked her away, casting an angry look at the daring young man. "That boy will be your ruin!" she hissed as she dragged Carmela inside the church.

***

Carmela's mode of attending the novenas was unlike those of the other ladies that showed up at the prayer meetings. Instead of entering with a bowed head and seeking to join the other attendees as they gathered before the altar, she rushed to the back row and sat alone, silently looking at the ceiling while the priest led the faithful in their prayers. An attentive observer could only conclude that the girl was marking time while the devotions ran their course.

It was not long before her behavior was noted by the ladies and became the subject of gossip among the village women, one of whom – a friend of Cecilia – referred obliquely to the peculiar praying habits of the youngest of the Serranos during the next sewing club meeting. She did not claim that there was anything wrong with Carmela's behavior, but the girl "seemed to be consumed by some private concern that was unusual for anyone so young and of such a good family."

Cecilia questioned her daughter sternly, suspecting some romantic entanglement, but Carmela was adamant in her denials. Yet the girl didn't sound sincere. So, Cecilia pressed Yaya for answers. "You are supposed to be looking after Carmela's well-being and don't seem to be doing too good a job at it," she charged the slave. At first, Yaya denied that there was anything irregular about Carmela's behavior, but when Cecilia posed the direct question "She's seeing a boy, isn't she?" Yaya could not continue covering up for her ward. "It's nothing like that…" she started, but Cecilia cut her off: "Who's he?" Yaya stammered something unintelligible, so Cecilia pressed: "The name, Yaya! Tell me his name!"

"It's Rodolfito, the boy who danced with her at her quince."

Cecilia remained silent for a moment, stunned, and then exploded: "That ruffian? What has he done to my daughter? Have you left him be alone with Carmela?!"

"Miss Cecilia, nuthin' has happened, as Holy Mary is my witness!" She stopped for a second to catch her breath and continued: "They sit outside the church for a few minutes on Friday nights, just before the novena, and chat! Nuthin' else!"

"How long has his going on?"

"Three or four weeks, I swear!"

"I have a mind to have Leonardo put you up for sale at the next market in Manzanillo!"

"Please, miss, nuthin' has happened!"

"Nothing, eh?" barked Cecilia. "My daughter's honor compromised! And with a common delinquent, a good for nothing vagrant off the streets! I'll have you whipped!"

"Miss, please punish me all you want, but do nuthin' to Carmelita, she's a good girl and has done nuthin' wrong, I swear!!"

Cecilia raised her arm to strike the slave but held herself in check. "I'll be the judge of that! Give me the details and tell me everything!"

***

Later that day, Cecilia had a tense confrontation with her daughter.

"You lied to me, and worse yet, you are hanging out with that scum! What were you thinking?!"

"Rodolfo is no scum, but a very decent man, and I like him a lot."

"He and his brother ruined the party we put so much effort into setting up for you! How can you be friends with him after that?!"

"Well, I'm sorry about the party, but it was not his fault. If Uncle Leonardo had not gotten so worked up, everything would have been fine!"

"And you still defend him! What has gotten into you?!"

"Nothing, mother! He's nice and smart and treats me like a grownup, which is more than you and Uncle do around here!"

"Well, I forbid you to see him again!"

"I'm old enough to decide who to see."

"I said and I meant it! Stop meeting that Rodolfito, or else…"

"What? Besides keeping me a prisoner in this dump, what else can you do to me?"

"You'll see…"

Chapter 9

Pilón, July, 1859: Confrontation

I didn't want anybody seeing my fire until I burned them with it.
Cameron Conaway

After her temper subsided, Cecilia examined her options and realized there were few. It was her fault that her children were confined to this backwater with no opportunities to make connections with people of any social significance. Carmela did not have much to choose from, after all. She had to take her children back to La Habana.

But, for the moment, she needed to make sure her daughter did not ruin her life by having an affair with someone from the gutter. She had to nip this romance in the bud.

She was reluctant to get her brother-in-law involved in this mess, but she knew Carmela. She was impulsive and stubborn as a mule. Punishing her would not work. They had to pull this weed by its roots.

"You are not going to believe this" she said to Leonardo, barging into his sugar mill office as he was ill-humored going through some bills. "What now?" he asked with some asperity.

"That boy that crashed our party for Carmela and created that big mess is bothering my daughter again."

Leonardo dropped the papers he was reading and gave a startled look to his sister-in-law. "Bothering how?"

"I don't know, stalking her on the way to church, trying to draw her into conversation. He apparently has not given up on her."

"The bastard!" Leonardo got up from his chair abruptly, causing it to tumble to the floor. "Don't worry, sister. Leave it up to me. I'll have a chat with the squirt!"

***

At dawn the following day, Leonardo and two of his bodyguards descended on a one-room shack at the edge of town near the foot of the mountains. Instead of knocking on the door, Leonardo yelled angrily: "Come out, cabrones, we want to talk to you!"

There was no response, and Leonardo directed his men: "Break the damn door down!" With savage kicks, the men tore the door off its hinges and sent it tumbling into the humble dwelling.

Rodolfito was not there. Rino, freshly awoken from sleep, stood against the back wall, waving a cattle branding iron, a scowl on his face. "Come on, hijos de la gran puta, come and get it!"

Neither Leonardo nor his men were armed and, instead of entering the shack, stood at the doorway. Leonardo questioned the boy angrily: "Where is your brother?"

"None of your goddamn business!" spat back Rino. Then he added: "He's at work."

"Tell him that if I hear again that he has been bothering my niece Carmela, I'll break every bone in his body, and yours, too!"

"Why don't you try that now. I'm here waiting for you!"

"Naw, we'll be back" replied Leonardo, waving his men away.

"You are goddamn cowards, and I'll take on any one of you mano a mano, any day you dare come by!" were Rino's parting words.

Leonardo glowered but turned his back on the shack and filed away with his men.

***

Late that night, unidentified persons threw burning, rum-soaked rags at the shack, whose palm-frond roof immediately caught fire. The shack burned to the ground in only a few minutes.

Rodolfo was able to get out with only minor burns. Rino was slow getting up from his slumber and was severely burned.

Chapter 10

Pilón, July, 1859: Convalescence

That which does not kill us makes us stronger.
Friedrich Nietzsche

Rino would have died had it not been for the intervention of Arturo Galván, the blacksmith for whom Rodolfo worked. Galván took it upon himself to transport Rodolfo and a delirious Rino to Pilón's tiny urgent care cottage at the edge of town run by the Sisters of Charity. There, the three nuns in charge of the facility gave their full attention to the burned boy and his grieving brother.

Sister Simona, who ran the facility, developed an instant liking for Rodolfo and, after the first couple of days, delicately broached the subject of the boys' future. "You should not have been by yourselves to start with. I can help place you and your brother, once he recovers, in an orphanage in Santiago."

Rodolfo reacted strongly to the suggestion. "Sister, we'll be eternally grateful to you and Sisters Alina and María de los Angeles for the care you have given us, but I'd rather die than lose my freedom, and I am sure Rino feels the same way. I already have an occupation and would very much like to continue to ply my trade as a blacksmith in this area."

"It would be very irregular for us to assist two minors to remain outside the bounds of the law; you belong in an orphanage, at least for the next couple of years."

"Sister, you would undo the great help you have given us by confining us to a place where we don't belong. We've been functioning in the world for the last two years and can't be considered children in need of care anymore. If those criminals had not set our home afire, we would still be managing rather well here in Pilón."

Sister Simona remained silent for a long while. Finally, she chose what she felt was the safest course of action.

"We have been working at this clinic only a short time and are not familiar with the general population of this area. Sister Alina, however, is from the Manzanillo area north of here and may know of a family there that would be willing to accept you two as their wards for the next couple of years. I will seek her counsel."

"But Sister…"

"We'll take this up again a bit later. In the meantime, go visit with your brother. He can use the company."

***

That afternoon, Sister Simona came to the room where Rodolfo was sitting next to the pallet where Rino rested. As she entered, she could hear the wounded boy's agitated voice: "I tell you I'll kill that bastard Serrano! With my own hands! He'll have to pay for this!"

"Shh…" cautioned Sister Simona. "No such words may be uttered in the place dedicated to Our Lord. Hush."

"Look at my face!" demanded Rino. "I bet I will have scars the rest of my life!"

"Talk about taking another man's life is not Christian. If you did that, it would be more than your face that would burn in Hell!"

Rino was about to utter a retort, but the nun continued: "Hush. Sister Alina here has an idea that might solve your problem, at least for the short run."

Sister Alina, a demure young woman, approached the pallet and spoke to both youths: "My uncle Manolo owns a small farm on the banks of the river Yara, not far from Manzanillo. I can write him and ask whether he would be willing to employ two young men as farmhands and serve as their guardian. Would you like me to do that?"

"How long would it take to hear back from your uncle?" asked Sister Simona.

"We send a rider to get our post to Manzanillo twice a week, coming back the following day. I could ask Carlos to make a side trip to Yara and get word from my uncle the same day. So, we would have the answer in three or four days."

"Please write to your uncle tonight. We will send the letter with Carlos tomorrow and have the answer by the end of the week" ordered Sister Simona. Anticipating an objection from one or both brothers, she added "you boys can't turn down an offer until you get it. Plus, you are going nowhere in the next few days anyways."

***

The answer came back in the form of a letter from Sister Alina's aunt: "Dear Alina: Your uncle is busy finishing the spring harvest and is not much of a writer, so I'm responding to your letter on his behalf as well as mine. This house is empty since our son left us to serve in the Spanish army. We would not mind having some young faces around to brighten our days. The work is hard, and we can't pay much, but we would welcome those two unfortunate children to come live with us and stay as long as they need. Please warn them that we are humble people and so is our home, but they will always have a good sancocho for dinner at the end of the day. Please send word back to us whether they will be coming and, if so, when. May our Lady of Charity bless you and keep you in good health. Love, Your Aunt Isabel."

***

"I'm not doing that" was Rino's emphatic response to the proposal. We are not guajiros, our life is in this town, not on a sitio like former slaves. Plus, I have a score to settle in Pilón and am not moving anywhere until I'm done."

Rodolfo's feelings were very much the same, but he had a practical side that helped him consider the situation they faced. "Listen, I don't like the idea any more than you do, but we are in a bind. You need to get better and recover your strength, and we need to plan how we are going to get our lives back. I say we go to that farm for a few weeks and then we'll see."

The decision was made for them through a visit from Sister Simona the following day. She went right to the point: "Listen, boys, we need for you to move on. As you know, this is a small facility, and we have other sick people requiring attention. Rino is sufficiently recovered from the worst of his burns to be able to get out of here. What are you going to do about the offer from Sister Alina's family?"

Rodolfo responded: "Are you trying to get rid of us?"

The nun blushed slightly. "It's not that. I don't feel you are safe around here. Whoever carried out this terrible crime may not stop and may come back to finish you off."

"Mother…" started Rino, but his brother cut in: "Sister, we are grateful for the offer, and we are inclined to accept it."

"I'll have Carlos deliver word when he goes to Manzanillo tomorrow. We'll borrow a cart, and he can drive you both to Yara once he comes back."

***

While they waited for Carlos to return, Rodolfo went to see Sister Simona. "Sister, I must ask you for a big favor. I need you to deliver a letter for me."

41

"To whom?"

"The letter is to be delivered to Yaya, the cook for the Serrano family."

"You are writing an old slave a letter?"

"It's not for her… but someone else."

"I see. Why don't you deliver it yourself?"

"You've said it before. I will be in danger if I show my face in public in this town."

"Still, we should not get involved in your affairs, which I suspect are rather dubious."

"Sister, I beg you! I agreed to go to Yara and talked my brother into doing the same, but I can't leave without sending a farewell letter to someone."

"That's even worse. Are you trying to make me into a procuress, a vulgar Celestina? Have you no shame?"

Rodolfito broke into tears. "Sister Simona, there is nothing illicit in the letter I am writing. You can even read it yourself to decide whether to deliver it. But please, I have nobody else to whom I can turn."

"Still, I don't think it is right for us to be involved."

"Well, I will have to do it myself then. I will go to the market tomorrow and hand it to Yaya. If something happens to me, it will be on your conscience!"

"Alright. Write the letter and show it to me. If I think it is prudent to do so, I will have Sister Maria de los Angeles take it to market tomorrow and hand it to that Yaya, if she can be found."

***

"My much-esteemed Carmela,

Due to circumstances of which you are aware, my brother and I must leave Pilón for some time. I don't know when I will be able to return, but rest assured that I will be back, and that I hope to resume our friendship at that point. Please think of me as well as you can. I will always carry your memory in my heart.

Until next we see each other, be well.

Affectionately,
Your servant,
Rodolfo Durán"

Chapter 11

Yara, July - August, 1859: A new Life

Coarse rice to eat, water to drink, my bended arm for a pillow –
therein is happiness.
Confucius

*L*ife was hard in *Los Suspiros*, the farm owned by the Galáns in Yara at the foot of the mountains. Manuel ("Manolo") and his wife Isabel worked from before dawn to after dusk attending to crops, raising pigs and goats, getting products ready for the market, and attending to the thousand chores that are required day to day in a small farming operation like theirs. They had two male slaves who assisted with the toughest jobs such as clearing the woods, cutting the cane in the plot devoted to support sugar production, and tilling the fields, but the owner had to do everything else.

Coffee beans were the farm's main crop. The ripe cherries had to be plucked from the branches of the coffee trees, often requiring workers to clear the area surrounding the trees and then reach up; the repeated operation often caused muscle strains, particularly for those–like Rodolfo and Rino–who had not performed such work before. Spending hours in the sun was exhausting and left the *cortadores* tired and irritable. Rodolfo was used to working hard before, but blacksmithing indoors was entirely different from outdoor labor on a farm.

The brothers reacted in different ways to the demands of living as fugitives in an isolated sitio. Rodolfo, ever polite, did his best to ingratiate himself with those that had offered him shelter. Isabel was taken with the boy, whose dark looks reminded her of her faraway son, and soon was treating him like another member of the family. Rino, on the other hand, was standoffish and barely civil to the Galáns, and made no effort to hide his anger and the pain at the burns that covered his face and much of his body. Only the influence of Rodolfo's exemplary behavior, plus Isabel's pity at his condition, saved him from being shown the door.

Matters came to a head four weeks after their arrival in Yara. It was a hot, humid August morning that promised to be a scorcher. As they finished their breakfast, Manolo announced: "We need to move harvesting to the area at the eastern edge of the property, for the cherries there were close to ready for picking yesterday and should be gathered today before they spoil."

Rodolfo said nothing, but Rino voiced a loud protest: "That sucks! That hillside is steep and hasn't been cleared by Domingo and Eusebio, so we'll spend the day like lumberjacks and will catch heatstroke. No way!"

Manolo gave him an icy stare and replied: "I think you are recovered enough to at least do some berry picking. You *will* go work on that hill…"

As they were about to take off, Manolo drew Rodolfo aside: "Un momento, Rodolfito."

Rodolfo knew what was coming and sighed.

"Rodolfito, you know we are fond of you and happy to have you with us. But your brother has a very bad attitude, and I have a mind to send him packing, so you better have a word with him. He needs to change his ways."

"Don Manuel, you know how grateful we are for your giving us shelter in our difficult situation. Things have been tough on Rino, and he can't get over the injustice of being the victim of a terrible injury and on top of that, being driven out of town. I'll speak to him tonight."

The promised talk never took place, however. The day's

work on the new hill was truly exhausting, and by the time the boys came back from the field they were dripping with sweat, their faces red like ripe mangoes. They had a quick dinner and collapsed on their cots.

Shortly before dawn, something disturbed Rodolfo, who tossed and turned for a few moments but finally sat up, rubbing sleep from his eyes. As he looked around the room, his brother's cot was empty.

"That jerk ran away with our mule" bellowed Manuel a bit later. "And he took all the food Isabel had left in the pantry, and my shotgun! Desgraciado!

Chapter 12

Manzanillo, August, 1859: Impatience

Anxiety does not empty tomorrow of its sorrows,
but only empties today of its strength.
Charles Spurgeon

$\mathcal{M}$anolo announced he was driving his cart to Manzanillo to report the theft of his mule and shotgun to the local alguacil. "If that crazy boy commits a crime using my gun, I don't want the blame to fall on my shoulders. Plus, I want my mule and weapon back!"

"Could I please ride with you?" begged Rodolfo. "I must get back to Pilón to catch my brother before he does something really bad."

Manolo obliged. "Take your things with you. You'll always be welcome at our house, but I don't want to see your brother ever again."

"I'm so sorry…" began Rodolfo, but he could not go on. His eyes welled with tears.

***

They arrived in Manzanillo in the early afternoon, and Rodolfo stationed himself outside the feed store, which also served as mail center for the area. He was hoping to find someone who was willing to take him down to Pilón in exchange for a few coins that a tearful Isabel had given him as he left Yara. There were no takers; the closest anyone would be able to take him was Niquero, another small town about a five day walk from Pilón. He had no money to buy a mule or a donkey, if one could be found for sale in Niquero, and his need was too urgent to attempt traveling on foot.

Sunset was drawing near, and Rodolfo's desperation was increasing when a familiar sight caught his eye: Carlos' cart, drawn by Raquel the nag, was plodding its way up the road north from Niquero.

Rodolfo began waiving wildly at the approaching vehicle, which eventually stopped right in front of him. Carlos dismounted and greeted the boy:

"Hey, Rodolfito! What you doin' here?"

"Hi, Carlos. I'm so happy to see you!" Without further explanation, Rodolfo blurted: "You must take me back to Pilón right away!"

"Well, I migh do dat, if you are really nice to me." The Black man smiled broadly and went on: "But it'll be tomorrow, after I pick up the mail for the Sisters and run some errands."

"Can those things wait a couple of days? I've got a real emergency!"

"No, mah boy. For one thing, I'm plumb tired and need to get some rest before heading back, and so does poor Raquel. I also need to get them some medications fixed for the cottage, and dat will take time. Sister Simona would skin me alive if I showed up without them medications."

"Oh, God, I really need to go right now…!"

"What's dem rush?"

"It's my brother Rino. He's off to Pilón himself, and is up to no good!"

"I sorry to hear dat. But the best I can do is rush back in the morning."

Rodolfo began biting his knuckles but finally relented: "Alright. We'll go back early tomorrow. It's all in God's hands!"

Chapter 13

Pilón, August, 1859: All Hell Has Broken Loose

Pride and excess bring disaster for man.
Xun Kuang

𝒯he nuns at the urgent care cottage were a bit alarmed when Raquel brought the cart down the muddy street at an unusually fast pace for an old nag. The animal was panting loudly from prolonged exertion.

The trip normally took about ten hours over the unreliable road (a dirt track that often turned quite muddy) and Carlos typically drove back from Manzanillo after breakfast, so he normally arrived in Pilón after sunset. Yet it was barely merienda time, mid-afternoon. Something strange was going on.

As the cart arrived, the nuns noticed that Carlos was not traveling alone. Next to him on the bench was Rodolfo Durán. "What is he doing here?" asked Sister Simona to no one in particular. "We went to a lot of trouble to get them out of town to protect them!"

She was about to ask the same question to Rodolfo when he anticipated her:

"Sister Simona, I need your help. My brother has gone crazy and came down here armed with a shotgun. I'm afraid he's gonna do something terrible!"

The nun turned pale and stood silent for a moment. Then her face set in a rigid mask. "Do you have any idea where he may be headed?"

"My guess is that he is gone to the sugar mill's manor house. He's convinced that Leonardo Serrano is behind the attack that left him all burnt up. He may be seeking revenge against Serrano."

Sister Simona's reaction was frenzied: "You need to stay here with us until things get sorted out. If you are out on the street, you may get arrested or hurt. I will send word to the alguacil. Carlos, go out right now to the police station and tell Alvarez that we have gotten word that Rinaldo Durán, the kid whose house got burned last month, is back in town, is armed, and may be going around the manor house. Don't mention that his brother is also in town."

Without a word, Carlos turned around, jumped back on the cart, and yanked on Raquel's reins to get the horse moving again to the equine's discomfort.

***

Even before he approached the manor house, Carlos noticed that trouble was brewing. Half of the town's inhabitants were on the streets, milling around and talking loudly with one another. Carlos caught snippets of the conversations:

"Did they catch him?"

"They say he is hiding in the woods!"

"How is Don Leonardo?"

"It's so awful! And Ruperto had three small children! What is poor Eulalia going to do?"

Carlos could not reach the mill's gate because an excited mob was gathered in front of it. He got off Raquel and asked to a man standing by: "What happened here?" There were several overlapping answers, but after a while he was able to discern that at dawn, someone had entered the mill compound through the open gate, marched to the manor house, shot Rupert as he stood guard at the front door, and fired through the dining room glass window at the Serrano family having breakfast, striking both Cecilia and Leonardo. She had sustained only a shoulder wound, but a bullet hit Leonardo in the stomach, and he was in serious condition. A startled Albertico had identified a fleeing Rinaldo Durán as the marksman.

Carlos wasted no time in further investigations. He got back in the cart and hastily returned to the urgent care cottage, finding all three nuns and Rodolfo standing outside, clearly waiting for him. "I'm sorry, Sor Rosario, I didn't get to warn Alvarez because there was no need." Facing Rodolfo, Carlos continued accusingly: "Your brother shot the Serranos and is on the lam!"

Sister Simona replied evenly: "We know. Right after you left Alvarez and his two aides came here looking for Rodolfo's brother. Luckily, we spotted him just as he was tying up his horse and hid Rodolfo in the back room. Alvarez told us what had happened, and I told him that Rino had not been seen here in weeks, so he darted off."

Carlos got off the cart and motioned towards the trough, ready to water Raquel. Sister Simona warned: "Raquel and you better get some rest. First light tomorrow you'll need to make an emergency trip to Yara!"

Chapter 14

Pilón - Yara, August, 1859: A Quick Return

As long as you are in my life, I will continue to love you with the hope that you will someday return the unconditional love I feel for you.
Alyssa Perkins

"**B**ut I've got to help my brother!" protested Rodolfo.

"If you stay around here, they'll most likely get you before you find Rino!" countered Sister Simona sternly. "Go back to the farm, we'll send word if we learn anything. Rino has broken the law and sooner or later he'll feel the garrote around his neck." The nun put her arm over the boy's heaving shoulder and added softly: "Go to the back room and try to catch a few winks. You need to be out of here before anyone spots you. If they do, at a minimum you will end up in an institution."

"I haven't done anything!" continued the young man.

"Leonardo Serrano is a very powerful man. Whether he lives or dies, you and your brother are going to become targets of the revenge of his supporters. You need to be as far from here as possible, right away."

"But I don't want to go…" repeated Rodolfo.

"You have even less of a choice than when we sent you away last month. Get away or get killed or sent to an orphanage."

Rodolfo tried to continue resisting, but he was too weary. He turned around and retreated to the sick room.

Just before dawn, Sister Simona went to wake him up. He was dressed and sitting on the cot, holding a crumpled piece of paper. "You need to do this for me, again!" he begged.

"Another letter for Carmela Serrano?" questioned the nun, incredulously.

"Yes. Promise that you will have it delivered to Carmela's slave, or I'll have to do it myself."

Sister Simona again knew she had no choice. If Rodolfo set foot in the market, it would be his end. Silently, she picked up the paper and read:

> *"Dear Carmela,*
>
> *I have no words to tell you how sorry I am for the terrible deed my brother has committed against your mother and uncle. Please believe me, I had nothing to do with it, it was a senseless act of revenge on Rino's part. I must go away again, without even having been able to see you. As I said earlier, I do not know when, but I will be back. I love you, and some day, God permitting, I will make you my wife. Please think of me without anger.*
>
> *Until next we see each other. I love you more than words can express.*
>
> *Yours,*
> *Rodolfo"*

***

Manolo and Isabel were taken aback by Rodolfo's sudden return to *Los Suspiros*, but tried to offer some consolation to the youth, whose face was a desolate mask of exhaustion, concern, and regret. "I meant what I said about your being welcome back here" insisted Manolo. "But we are all going to have to work extra hard. We are shorthanded and I need to buy a new mule … and another shotgun."

Chapter 15

Pilón, August, 1859: A Divided Family

All happy families resemble one another,
but each unhappy family is unhappy in its own way.
Leo Tolstoy

*T*he **Serranos presented** a common front to the world in the aftermath of the attack that wounded Cecilia and left Leonardo on the verge of death. The mother, physically hurting and morally outraged, condemned Rino's attack as an unforgivable non-Christian act. "They should shoot that bastard on sight and spare the town the trouble of a trial," she would repeat to anyone within earshot. The children outwardly concurred with their mother, adding to their grievances against Rino a concern for her recovery from the shoulder wound.

Indoors, however, their unanimity fractured. Graciela had little interest in family affairs, but was loyal to her mother and was genuinely outraged that someone would dare to shoot at them. Alberto felt guilty about indirectly unleashing the chain of events that had led to the attack on Rino and his revenge, but sympathized with his former friend's rage, though could not condone the attack on his uncle. Carmela was the sole dissenter: her uncle had brought the shooting on himself by the cowardly assault that left Rino scarred for life. "Leonardo is a prick and deserved what he got" she would start, and usually end, sharp arguments with her mother.

The dispute festered with the passage of time, for the authorities were unable track down the criminal despite sending search parties through a good part of the Sierra Maestra's western mountains. Meanwhile, Leonardo's condition showed no improvement: the bullet had lodged near the spine, and it was not feasible to operate to remove it. He remained an invalid, suffering from a great deal of pain and unable to continue to run the mill's affairs.

Cecilia would have moved back to La Habana and left Pilón and its sorrows behind, but Leonardo could not be moved without great risk to his life, and the mill–which now was being offered for sale–had to continue to operate, managed by her with the assistance of Leonardo's secretary, who was the mill's administrator. It was an uneasy paralysis, which aggravated the conflict among the family members.

One evening as they shared another unenjoyable meal, Graciela made an announcement: "Living in this house is not pleasant anymore. I'm going to move in with my friend Ernestina Cueto. They have a spare room in their home, and I will enjoy the company of the Cuetos better than the funeral atmosphere here."

"You didn't ask whether I approved of such move, which I don't think is appropriate under the circumstances."

"Mother, I am eighteen years old. I need no permission to move anywhere I damned please."

"Don't you dare challenge your own mother!" warned Cecilia, raising her voice.

"I will, if that's what it takes to become independent."

"Graciela, decent girls only leave their homes to get married. What you are talking about doing would be a scandal. You would add shame to all the grief our family is going through right now," the mother wailed.

"How and where I live is nobody's business. I'm not going to let the gossips in your sewing circle rule my life."

"Well, if you choose to leave, don't count on getting any support from me!"

"I don't need your money. I still have the trust that father set up for me before he died a decade ago. When that runs out, or even before, I will get a job to support myself."

"A job? Like the peons? A girl of a good family working? Out on the streets like a puta?"

"I'm no whore. I can get a job as a teacher any day I want. God knows the schools in this dump of a town could use somebody qualified to teach letters to the local boys and girls."

"Well, do as you want. I have no time to deal with your caprice."

"Don't worry, I will."

Chapter 16

Pilón, September, 1859: Finding a New Friend

Each new friendship can make you a new person
because it opens up new doors inside of you.
Kate DiCamillo

Alberto spent some time searching through Pilón's young male population for more reliable friends than the disappeared Durán brothers. His efforts proved, for the most part, unsuccessful. Most of the town's teenage population consisted of barely educated or illiterate members of the lower classes, already earmarked for a brutish life as farm hands or laborers at the mill.

There was one notable exception, however: Carlos Rafael ("Carlitos") Masó, a descendant of a family of means that owned a large farm in Yara. Carlos and his mother had moved to Pilón when she separated from her husband Rafael on account of his frequent infidelities and lived off an inheritance she had received from her father. Mother and son were reasonably well-to-do; Carlitos was an alert and pleasant young man who was well above Alberto's usual football-playing buddies.

Alberto and Carlitos met by accident during one of Alberto's excursions to the mountains that rose behind the town. Alberto was following his favorite trail, climbing sharply towards the mountain peaks, when, taking a sudden turn of the road, he nearly collided with another boy who stood in the middle of the path watching intently the woods above through a pair of binoculars.

"Pardon me" apologized Alberto. "I did not expect running into anyone way out here."

"No problem" replied Carlitos. "I come here whenever I can to watch the birds."

"What birds?" asked Alberto, who was largely ignorant of the wildlife of the Sierra Maestra.

"All kinds of birds!" replied Carlitos enthusiastically. "There are always dozens of birds flying around this area. See?" He handed to binoculars over to Alberto and pointed to a tall pine that rose across the trail. On the irregular crown of the tree was perched a spectacular bird with blue and white feathers and a deep red chest that sat placidly but, from time to time, uttered a pleasant "toco-toco-tocoro-tocoro…" call.

"Coño, que lindo" declared Alberto. "What's it called?"

"They call it a tocororo because of the way it sings," replied Carlitos. "And that's not the only nice bird you can see…"

***

That chance encounter evolved into a solid friendship. The two boys, who were of similar age (Carlitos was just one year older than Alberto), had similar interests in literature, sports, and music, and both were starting to think about girls and wonder about their future. As they became more trusting of one another, they discovered they had another, potentially more dangerous interest in common. Since he had witnessed as a young boy Narciso López's execution Alberto had been dissatisfied with the oppressive Spanish rule of its last major colony in the Americas; Carlitos had confided that he harbored similar feelings.

"Why don't you come with me to Manzanillo sometime?" asked Carlitos one afternoon. "Mom sends me there every once in a while, to spend time with my father and my two uncles, Bartolomé and Isaías."

"What's in Manzanillo for me?" queried Alberto.

"It is a nice town. And it has a new logia."

"What's a logia?"

"It's like a social club. I can't tell you more, because I don't exactly know. I'm not old enough to join, but my father and uncles are members and speak highly of their logia, although they don't discuss the details of what they do."

"But if you are too young to belong, so am I," objected Alberto.

"But you can still come visit my folks and hear some interesting things."

"Well, it seems rather mysterious, but I would go, just to keep you company. When are you going?"

"Next couple of weeks. I'll let you know."

***

The *Tropical Star No. 4* Masonic Lodge was too small and recently established to have a permanent site. Its couple of dozen members were all male, educated, reasonably well-to-do residents of the coastal area of the Santiago de Cuba province that ran from the mouth of the Cauto River to Cabo Cruz. Most resided in or around Manzanillo. For that reason, the Lodge's meetings took place in a private room in Manzanillo's largest tavern.

Neither Carlitos (age 15) nor Alberto (14) would be allowed to attend November's meeting of the Manzanillo Lodge. However, they stayed at the tavern as guests of Rafael Masó, Carlitos' father, and sat through the backroom discussion the three brothers held–assisted by large amounts of Rioja–concerning the political issues that were brought up during the meeting. Bartolomé, as usual, led the discussion:

"I must be the only one around here that is pessimistic about the change in governor. It is perhaps good that Prime Minister O'Donnell decided to replace butcher Concha with his protégé Francisco Serrano (not related to Alberto's family), but I doubt that the new governor will be any better for Cuba than his predecessor. All that Madrid cares for is bleeding us dry and whoever is in charge here will only implement the dictates of the Court."

Alberto did not follow the details of the discussion that ensued, but he remembered well that Concha had been governor when Narciso López had attempted to invade Cuba. Concha had quashed the invasion and put López and the other conspirators to death by garrote, a gruesome event that had been engraved in Alberto's memory. Serrano, whoever he was, had to be an improvement over Concha.

Something about the conversation, however, stayed with Alberto: the people who belonged to this Lodge were passionate about how their land was ruled and what the future held for them and the rest of the inhabitants of Cuba. He had never contemplated becoming involved in politics as a part of his life, but now realized that in the future, it would be as important, perhaps, as playing ball or gazing at pretty girls.

Chapter 17

Pilón, December, 1859: Holiday Cheer

Christmas is not a time or a season but a state of mind.
Calvin Coolidge

*C*hristmas that year was a joyful holiday for many people in Pilón. With the growth in the sugar industry, economic conditions were good despite the poor administration of the colonial government. Salaries and the Christmas holiday bonus allowed the sugar mill workers to have a plentiful feast for their special Nochebuena dinner: the smell of roasting pork permeated throughout town.

The Serrano family was holding a holiday reception on Christmas Eve. Cecilia was not in the mood for celebrations but felt obliged to invite the families of the key mill employees in addition to public officials (all Spaniards, as government jobs at all levels tended to be). Wine and hard liquors flowed freely and hired servers made the rounds offering pastelitos de carne (meat pastries), crab croquettes, deviled ham sandwiches, and other delicacies, while a hired string quartet played the latest light music straight from Vienna. Cecilia circulated around the salon chatting with the guests while her daughters, enlisted for the occasion, spent time talking with the younger members of the visitors. Christmas Eve was supposed to be a day of fasting, but everyone in Cuba skirted the ecclesiastical command by feasting and serving dinner late that evening, after which many of the faithful (mostly the ladies) would take a leisurely walk to help digest their dinner. They would proceed to the church where they would sit through the Misa del Gallo, the midnight mass ushering in Christmas day.

Carmela was chatting with some girls from their social circle when Yaya approached her and whispered, "Pardon me, my lady, but there is someone at the door asking for you." She was visibly upset.

"What's the matter?" asked Carmela, puzzled.

Yaya did not respond but walked quickly to the front door and opened it slightly. Rodolfo Durán, pale as a ghost, took a step forward but did not seek to enter the house.

"Rodolfo!" exclaimed Carmela, "What in heaven are you doing here?"

"I've come to get you" he declared in a voice that broke.

"What do you mean?"

"I figured that tonight, of all nights, everyone else would be busy with other things and it would be safe for me to come see you."

Carmela stepped out onto the front porch and confronted the boy. "What do you want? Don't you know the alguaciles have been looking for you and your criminal brother for months?"

"I don't know where Rino is" replied Rodolfo remorsefully. "But I live north of here, and don't plan to ever come back."

"Well, good, because you would not be welcome after what your brother did."

Rodolfo extended his arm and grasped Carmela's elbow. "Would you please walk with me for a few moments?"

Carmela demurred. "I'm busy tonight. We are entertaining half the town."

"I know, but this is important and can't wait. My life depends on it."

Carmela, used to Rodolfo's suicidal pronouncements, stepped onto the porch and then out into the street. "Alright. But we must be quick."

"I want you to marry me" blurted Rodolfo, without preamble.

"What? Have you lost your mind?"

"No. Listen. I have been working on a coffee plantation north of here. The owner died suddenly a few days ago and his widow, whose son has moved permanently to Europe, does not want to sell the farm and has offered me to become her partner and assume responsibility for the plantation's operations. It is a lot of work, but I will be making good money for the foreseeable future." He paused to catch his breath.

"What does that have to do with me?" asked Carmela coldly.

"Now I can afford to provide you with a comfortable life, just like you deserve."

There was a pause while Carmela tried to digest the new information. "So, you are saying that you feel you can now support me properly. Therefore, I should marry you?"

"Exactly!"

"What makes you think I would want to marry you, even if you offered me a castle in Spain?"

"Because I love you, I know you at least like me, and I know you are not happy living with your shitty family!"

"Curb your tongue! I love my family!"

"You yourself have told me that you despise your uncle and don't get along with your mother or your sister. What's holding you here?"

"I have had differences with everyone but Albertico, but that doesn't mean I'm ready to bolt away."

"With me you would be able to do as you pleased and wouldn't have to feel guilty about the terrible things your uncle does. You would be able to start a new life, be your own person, be free! You'll never be able to do this as long as you live under that roof, and you will end up marrying a pot-bellied Gallego smelling of garlic who will treat you as a slave."

"You give me no credit for being able to fight for myself."

"And do what? You are a prisoner here in Pilón and will never escape."

"Come on" replied Carmela with irritation. "You exaggerate."

"You know in your heart I'm right."

There was another pause. They stood under a tallow lamp streetlight that cast a feeble, flickering illumination to the night. Despite the uncertain light, Rodolfo could notice how the expression on Carmela's face shifted from defiance to regret. Finally, she broke the silence. "Anyhow, the most important problem is that I don't love you. At best, you have been a friend. Nothing more."

Rodolfo could barely hide his smile. "But you do! How many times have we sat on that bench in the church's garden? How many times have you poured your soul into mine, and I trusted you with my all my wishes and fears?" He took her hand, and she did not pull back.

He caressed her hand and lowered his voice so it became a whisper. "You know I love you like nobody has before and never will. Trust your heart and come with me."

Carmela started to pull away to free herself, when an angry voice sounded behind them, by the front door: "Carmela, where are you and what are you doing?" It was Cecilia, summoning her daughter to return to give service at the party.

Carmela responded in the impulsive way of all her dealings with Rodolfo. "I've had it here! Let's go!"

Rodolfo led her into the night to the next corner where a lit lamp sat on the ledge of a building wall. He retrieved the lamp with one hand and led Carmela with the other.

"Where are we going?"

"To the church, where else? Father Pastor is waiting."

***

Father Pastor stood in the nave of the church in the company of his altar boys and a man that Carmela at first did not recognize. "Finally," the man remonstrated, and Carmela recognized him: it was Carlos, the Black slave who worked for the nuns that ran the emergency care unit. "Does your mistress know you are here?"

"I left for Manzanillo two days ago. As far as Sister Simona knows, I'm still there. When I return, I'll tell her that the cart lost a wheel, and it took me a long time to get it repaired."

"Will she believe you?"

"I hope she does. If not, I will be sold to some sugar cane farmer."

"Well, Father, it took some doing" said Rodolfo sheepishly. But we are here now!"

Father Pastor cleared his throat. "I didn't think this was going to happen. Let's not waste any more time. Sooner or later, someone is going to come looking for this girl. I want you out of here before they arrive."

The ceremony was brief. When it was over, the priest declared:

"I will probably be run out of town for this, but you are now man and wife. Love each other and be faithful. May the Lord bless your union." He made the sign of the cross and waved them away.

Carlos led the way to the back of the church building, where a mule and cart waited for them. "It's going to be a difficult drive, going out on the county road in the dark of night. I suggest we stop in Niquero until dawn and then proceed to Manzanillo in the morning."

"I have nothing, nothing!" complained Carmela bitterly as she mounted the cart.

"Don't worry, my dear. You are dressed nicely. We'll buy everything you need in Manzanillo," replied Rodolfo.

It was Carlos this time who repeated Yaya's refrain: "It's madness." And then he added: "But love often is."

Chapter 18

Pilón, December, 1859: Holiday Blues

*Christmas is a holiday that persecutes
the lonely, the frayed, and the rejected.*
Jimmy Cannon

*C*ecilia had ample reasons to feel down as the last week of the year came along. Carmela's elopement had filled her with anger and shame, and Graciela's final preparations to leave home were no less depressing for having been announced. Her brother-in-law remained bedridden and in critical condition, leaving her saddled with the task of running a large business, something for which she had no aptitude or interest. Only Albertico remained loyal and affectionate, but apart from his love he was too young to be useful to her at the moment.

She had contacted lawyers in La Habana, tasking them with securing a buyer for *Santa Cruz*. The sugar industry was still expanding wildly in Cuba, and the lawyers had assured her that she would be able to sell the mill and realize a good profit, but warned that finding a buyer or a group of investors with the means and interest in acquiring a property in the eastern end of Cuba might take some time.

Thus, Cecilia found herself almost alone in the drawing room of the manor house on New Year's Eve, waiting to say goodbye to that tumultuous year and hoping for better times to come.

Albertico sat next to her on the blue velvet divan. They were eating canapes and drinking champagne (for which the boy, not yet of age, had received a special dispensation). Before them, on a low table, sat a large bowl full of imported grapes. As the grandfather clock across the room from them ticked away the seconds that remained of the year 1859, Cecilia could no longer hold back her tears.

"How I missed your father, darling. If Lázaro had been alive, none of this would have happened! This family is in such a mess…!" She clutched her son to her breast. "Promise you will stay with me… you won't abandon me, the way your ungrateful sisters have!"

"Nunca, mamá! I'll always be by your side!" he promised.

The clock started striking the hour and Cecilia composed herself. "Come on, let's eat the grapes of good fortune! Make a wish for the new year!" She picked a grape, bit into it, and swallowed it in a single gulp.

Albertico did the same. They ate in silence, keeping their wishes to themselves, but hoping against hope that they would somehow come true.

Epilogue

Pilón, April, 1860: Welcome to the Sixties

The 1860s witnessed an extraordinary sequenceof developments.
Major conflicts rocked the Americas, Europe, South
Asia and partsof the Caribbean and the Pacific world.
Princeton University, Department of History –
The Global 1860s

On Palm Sunday, 1860, while Cecilia, Albertico, and all the help at the manor house were outdoors watching the traditional procession that ushered in Holy Week, Leonardo Serrano, addled by the medications he was taking to alleviate his pain and drawn by the noise outside, got up from his sick bed, took a few steps towards the window, and collapsed in a heap. The fall undid much of the mending that had taken place since the shooting and confined Leonardo to his bed and, later, required him to spend most of his time in an invalid chair imported from England at considerable expense.

Although physically debilitated, Leonardo had made enough of a recovery to reassume the reins of operating *Santa Cruz*. Even though the worldwide demand for cane sugar was starting to level off, he put a hold on Cecilia's attempts to sell the mill and asserted that the family—or what was left of it—would remain in Pilón for the foreseeable future. Cecilia accepted her brother-in-law's judgments partly out of pity for him but mostly to remain in the same town with Graciela and not too far from her ingrate daughter Carmela. Secretly, however, she made up her mind: when he became of age, she would send Albertico to La Habana for good to complete his studies and make a life and a future for himself.

"At least one of us will have a chance to lead a normal life" she kept repeating to herself. But, of course, she expected that with the new decade unexpected challenges would continue to rise for her and her scattered family. She could only hope that she and the children would be able to meet them.

Part 2

1865

Dark Clouds Gather

Prologue

Pilón, Oriente, May, 1863

Time is a great healer, but a poor beautician
Lucille S. Harper

Alberto Serrano got so drunk the night of his eighteenth birthday that his drinking companions had to drag him bodily all four blocks from the bar to the sugar mill's gate, where they left him in the hands of the guards. Ten minutes later, he was lying on his bed in the manor house, snoring in an alcoholic stupor.

The following afternoon, as Alberto tried to recover from the effects of his escapade, Cecilia sat next to her son on the drawing room's blue velvet divan. Although upset at the boy's behavior, she tried to put a positive cast on the situation. Alberto was the only one of her children who had remained with her through the last four years and had always proved to be well-behaved and dutiful.

"Did you have a good time celebrating with your friends?" she asked in a cheerful tone.

"Not really" replied Alberto, hiccupping.

"Why not?"

"Mother, I went drinking because I was bored, and I had to do something to mark coming of age. But I don't like rum and the guys I was with were not great company. I really miss Carlitos!"

"I know. Carlos Masó is a nice fellow and has been a good friend to you. Pity that he had to move to La Habana three years ago."

"He didn't have to go. His family sent him to La Habana to get an education there instead of going to Spain."

"Anyhow, I am sorry he wasn't around to share the occasion with you."

Alberto did not reply but stared at the carpet sullenly.

After a while, Cecilia put her hand on her son's shoulder. "Listen, Alberto, you know you have been my joy and support since the girls left. But I should not sacrifice your future for my benefit. You need to be like Carlitos and start thinking of what you are going to do with your life. I have paid for private tutors who have given you a basic education. I should send you now to Madrid to learn to be a businessman or a man of letters."

Alberto snapped back to attention. "To Madrid? Never. I hate the Spaniards here and would hate them there even more!"

"Well, Paris, then. Or the United States, but they are in the middle of a terrible war."

"I don't want to go abroad. I want to stay close to home so I can come back to you in case of need. You are here by yourself, with no company other than Uncle Leonardo, who is an invalid."

"How about Santiago?"

"Santiago is like Pilón, only bigger. I'm tired of living in a village, and I won't learn anything useful there."

It was not lost on Cecilia that her son was not rejecting the thought of leaving home, only quibbling over the destination. "How about going to La Habana? You grew up there and you could renew your ties with Carlitos."

Alberto's expression brightened. "That might not be a bad idea. I would not mind going to the university in La Habana."

He has been thinking about this already but was too shy

to tell me. So be it. "Let me look into it. We would need to find a good boarding house where you could live and pursue your studies."

"I will write Carlitos tonight!" declared Alberto, his mood considerably brighter.

***

Carlos Masó's response to Alberto's inquiry pointed out that the admission standards at the University of La Habana were fairly high, and Alberto might fail to get in, since the schooling Alberto had received in Pilón at the hands of Don Gerardo, his private teacher, had been rather superficial. He suggested that some preparatory courses would be a good idea:

"As you know, I attended the Normal School that was opened by the Piarist Fathers in Guanabacoa, a town not far from La Habana, to get qualified to attend the university. I will visit with my former teachers there and see if they can accept you as a special student to take college preparation courses. They may say no, or you may not be interested in doing what I suggest, but time is short and all that can happen is that I will have wasted a couple of hours."

***

While mother and son were having an amiable chat, in a farm some distance to the north another member of the family was carrying out a different conversation.

Carmela Serrano stood with her hands pressed against the dinner table, eyes glittering. "How could you do that to me? And how about your children, don't you have any respect for them?" She ran a hand nervously over the head of Rodolfito ("Fifo"), the oldest son sitting on a baby chair, and turned her sight to the cradle in the corner of the room where Lázaro, the youngest, slept placidly.

"I tell you again, Carmela, I've done nothing wrong!" protested Rodolfo Durán, Carmela's husband.

"Come on, stop lying! Ever since we hired Cristina to look after the kids you have not missed a chance to lay your paws on her!" Carmela's voice dropped an octave as depression joined anger in the cocktail of her emotions.

"Listen, Carmela. It was your idea, not mine, to hire a servant to help you with the house and the children. You know *Los Suspiros* is not doing all that well, but I went along because you are looking more ragged each day and I don't want you to get sick and die. Cristina is a nice girl, but I'm not attracted to her in the least."

"She is not a girl. She is a woman in her twenties, almost the same age as you and I. And, by the way, she is quite a flirt. She barely respects me, but hangs on your every word, as if you were the greatest invention since arroz con pollo. She wants something from you, I am sure. Ese huevo quiere sal, as my mother likes to say. I just can't stand it anymore!" Carmela broke down in a torrent of tears.

Rodolfo approached his wife and placed his arms around her heaving shoulders. "I'm sorry, my dear. When I took you away from your family, I thought life going forward would be easier for us, but making a success turned out much harder than I anticipated. Doña Isabel lives in retirement in Bayamo but is still part owner of this farm and half of what we make goes to her, leaving little for us to expand. I forced you to make sacrifices and change your life in ways to which you were not accustomed. I am to blame for all of that, but I am innocent of having carnal desires towards Cristina or anyone else. You are, and will always be, the only woman for me."

Husband and wife embraced, and Carmela's crying ceased little by little. But she was not done. "Well, show me that this is true. Fire Cristina and let's get an older woman to help around here."

Rodolfo frowned but raised no objection.

***

All was quiet that afternoon in the small house that Gracie-la Serrano and Ernestina Cueto owned on the outskirts of town. Graciela had just returned from her job as a teacher at Pilón's public school and was watching disinterestedly as Ernestina was preparing dinner. Ernestina was in charge of cooking and cleaning in the household, while Graciela – whose income supported the house's expenses – spent most of her time playing the piano; she had managed to buy copies of Chopin's Etudes Op. 10 and 25 and spent countless hours trying to master their difficulties, and writing poetry, at which she had become reasonably skilled.

That afternoon, she was trying to write a sonnet honoring the majesty of the Cauto river and was having trouble finding a rhyme for the word alturas (heights), so she asked her friend: "I'm stuck. Give me something that rhymes with alturas. With-out hesitation, Ernestina replied "basuras" (trash). Graciela's face contorted in a moue. "Uf," she objected. "How did you come up with such an ugly word?"

Ernestina was apologetic. "Sorry, my dear. I was thinking of your family, particularly your mother. You left Cecilia's house four years ago to move with me and in that span of time I don't think she has spoken to us more than two or three times. She treats you, I mean us, as if we were rubbish."

"Well, mother has problems. First, she is old school and narrow-minded. She can't approve of women living by them-selves, and even less in the company of other women unless they are nuns. Also, she is very sensitive to gossip and must have heard the rumors going around town about us. And she is quite religious, and thinks we are living in sin. So, she is a lost cause."

"How about Carmela and Alberto? I thought you got along fairly well with them, but we never see them either."

"Well, you know Carmela eloped with her boyfriend and went north to the Manzanillo area. I have not seen her since that time and don't miss her. As far as Albertico is concerned, I expect that if it were up to him, he would be friendly to us. But he lives with Cecilia and does nothing without her approval. So, I think he is also a lost cause."

"I am sorry if I am somehow to blame for your distancing from your family."

Graciela put her arms around Ernestina, embraced her tightly, and whispered: "Family. Who needs them? We have each other!" And she kissed Ernestina's ear tenderly.

Chapter 1

La Habana, September 1863: The Turbulent Sixties

The human bird shall take his first flight,
filling the world with amazement.
Leonardo da Vinci

Alberto returned to La Habana the same way his grandfather Lázaro had done eighty years earlier. Instead of traveling overland for weeks over unsafe and difficult roads, he took passage on a boat that sailed west from Santiago and then northwest, hugging Cuba's southern coast. One important difference, however, was that Lázaro had traveled on a galleon, and his grandson did so on a Confederate steamship that was running the blockade imposed by the United States on Southern ports. The trip was risky, for Union gunners patrolled the Caribbean waters seeking to capture rebel ships but the need to transport goods and mail to and from the Southern states also created the opportunity to move merchandise and passengers from one Cuban port to another.

He had traveled alone, rejecting Cecilia's plan to send one of the sugar mill's guards along as Alberto's escort. "Mother, if I am to grow into an adult, I must start acting as one without a chaperone or babysitter. Life is full of risks and I need to learn to deal with them myself." In the face of her son's strong stand,

Cecilia relented and resigned herself to letting him have his way.

When the steamship docked in La Habana, Alberto realized at once that the city he had left as a child seven years earlier had changed significantly. Astonishing economic growth had forced the ancient walls that had protected the town from pirates and foreign invaders to be taken down to accommodate the expansion of new business and dwelling areas. The immense wealth that had been gained from the sugar and tobacco industries was translated into palatial mansions and multi-story commercial establishments, and the boundaries of the city had expanded in all directions.

Alberto was able to see some of these changes as he traveled by horse-drawn tram from the port to his destination in the ancient town of Guanabacoa east of the harbor. Guanabacoa had a rich history: at one point in the mid fifteen hundreds it had been briefly Cuba's capital when La Habana was captured by French privateers; later, when the English launched their attack on La Habana during the Seven Year War, Guanabacoa had been a focus of resistance against the English troops, and Alberto's grandfather Lázaro had been a participant in the fight against the invaders.

What drew Alberto to Guanabacoa, however, was a more recent event. Six years earlier, in 1857, the town's former Convent of San Francisco had been turned into the first Normal School in Cuba. The school was founded and run by the Piarist Fathers, who ran similar institutions throughout Europe. Even though primarily intended to train future teachers, the school accepted, in exceptional cases, students like Carlos and Alberto who wished to enroll in the University of Habana but needed to round out the schooling they had received from private instructors.

With the help of his friend Carlos (who had made the personal contacts), Alberto had gained admission into the Escuelas Pías as a boarding student for a year on a trial basis.

The Guanabacoa school was part of an impressive complex that included a three-story main building featuring cells for the priests, housing for the out-of-town pupils who resided on campus, a huge kitchen and dining room, ample classroom space on the lower two floors, and a very large backyard which served as a playground as well as an exercise arena and was the site of outdoors school events. The most eye-catching part of the complex, however, was a cloister containing a lovely indoor garden, which held numerous specimens of domestic and foreign plants of all kinds. To the left, an off-white plain wall without windows led to the main entrance to the building, and at the other end lay the side entrance to the church.

Alberto was not particularly devout, but he felt in awe at the quiet majesty of the institution. I'll do well here, he promised himself.

Chapter 2

Pilón, Oriente, November 1863: Dissolution

It helps to walk away sometimes, even though it [may be] super hard.
Wiz Khalifa

*T*he ride to the family estate in Pilón proved much harder for Carmela than the late-night elopement from it had been. For one thing, now she was carrying her two young sons and considerably more baggage than when she had absconded with Rodolfo four years earlier. More significantly, perhaps, was her changed mood: then, she had been an impulsive teenager, drawn by anger at her family; now, disillusionment made the return trip bitter.

She knew that her mother would receive her with open arms and the welcome Cecilia would give her and her children would be free of recriminations. Nonetheless, she anticipated the disappointment that from now on would underlie all their interactions. Cecilia had disapproved of her friendship with Rodolfo and had been outraged at their secret wedding and scandalous flight; the letter Carmela had sent her mother announcing her impending return had been one of the few communications between them since she had left.

As the guards opened the gate to the *Santa Cruz* mill and the manor house Carmela felt an impulse to ask the driver to turn around, but it was too late. Cecilia had walked outside the mansion to stand on the road, ready to greet her daughter and grandchildren. The carriage came to a stop, the driver opened the door, and Carmela, hugging little Lázaro against her breast and leading Fifo by the hand, dismounted and walked towards her mother, both women crying incessantly.

"What made you decide to leave Rodolfo?" asked Cecilia as she escorted the arrivals into the house. She was tempted to reproach Carmela for her stupidity, but strove instead to keep a level tone to their discussion.

"It was a combination of things. He denied it, but I suspect he was cheating on me with the children's caretaker. I would have tried to put up with that, but I could no longer face the thought of my boys growing up in ignorance and misery. *Los Suspiros* barely produces enough coffee beans to pay our bills, and no matter how hard we work, there is never enough money left at the end of the month to do more than cover necessities. It just got to be too much, and I decided it was time to cut my losses and come back home."

***

Later, as they sat drinking small glasses of guarapo, Cecilia brought up a problem that was fresh in her mind: "You know, Leonardo is barely conscious these days. I have no head for business but needed to take control over the operation of *Santa Cruz* to prevent our underlings from bankrupting the mill. I wish he had let me sell the mill four years ago when the going was good."

"How's business?" asked Carmela disinterestedly.

"Things have gotten worse since you left. Spain is being required by the English to enforce the prohibition from importing slaves from Africa, so now we have to hire free Blacks and import Chinese workers to raise and harvest the cane and process it at the mill. That makes the refined sugar we make more expensive than what they produce in Brazil and other places."

Carmela interrupted with a question: "Don't they have the same problems with the lack of slave workers?"

"Yes, but they have started to mechanize the manufacturing

84

process, cutting labor costs. But Spain won't let us buy machinery from anywhere but the mother country, while its offerings are lower quality and more expensive. Plus, Spain still charges oppressive taxes on our operations while officially prohibiting us from selling directly on the world market. We need to charge more per sack of refined sugar than a mill in Pernambuco does."

"And what can we do?"

"As Mateo says, 'we need to modernize and economize. He tells me there are ways to work around Spain's laws, but they aren't easy.' I don't know how anyone does it."

"Ah! Is Mateo Ruiz still Leonardo's right-hand man at the mill?"

"Yes. We are lucky he is an honest man, but he is getting on in years. Plus, he is not too smart and constantly needs guidance."

"With Leonardo out of commission, who is going to provide such guidance?"

"You and I are."

Chapter 3

La Habana, May 25, 1864: A Fist Fight

*The kid in the schoolyard that doesn't want
to fight always leaves with a black eye.*
Curtis Jackson

Alberto's first year at the Escuelas Pías had gone well. His special status set him apart from nearly everyone else, but he was friendly and low-keyed and tried to stay away from the conflicts that raged between the two groups of students: those who were children of peninsulares, Spaniards who had been deployed to Cuba by the Government or had come to the island to make a fortune, and the offspring of local families, the criollos.

There was growing animosity between the two groups, because the rulers in Spain had for the centuries mandated that all positions of authority and influence in Cuba—from the Captain General (Governor) to the lowest postmaster—were to be filled by persons sent from Spain who treated the island as an orange to be squeezed for their benefit with little sympathy or respect for the local population. The criollos, many of whose families were wealthy enough to afford the high cost of education in private schools, resented the highhandedness of the peninsulares. They missed no chance to ridicule the strange accent and odd customs of the foreigners.

There was also an important cleavage on the issue of slavery. Most students at the Escuelas Pías opposed the continued existence of slavery as an institution and favored the recent prohibition on the importation of slaves captured in Africa; a few, however, came from families whose business in sugar, tobacco or coffee depended on slave labor. Alberto was torn on the issue, for he personally loathed the abuses to which slaves were subjected, but his family's wealth (some of which he someday would inherit) came from the ownership of a sugar mill that utilized scores of slaves for its operation.

The controversy over slavery boiled over when the Diario de la Marina reported the arrival in La Habana on May 23, 1864, of the U.S. steamship Eagle carrying aboard José Agustín Argüelles, the former military commander of the district of Colón. Argüelles had been deported by the United States at the request of Domingo Dulce, Cuba's Capitán General. Argüelles had led the police action that, acting on a tip, captured over one thousand shackled Black men (bozales) being illegally imported to serve as slaves in Cuban sugar mills. However, a discrepancy had been discovered between the number of Black men initially reported as liberated (over 1100) and the number transported to La Habana to be registered as free men (1000).

Argüelles was accused of keeping over 100 of the bozales he had seized, causing them to become enslaved. Julián Zulueta y Amondo, just appointed Mayor of La Habana, was the owner of the ship that had brought the bozales to Cuba and the purchaser of the entire lot. He was thirsting for revenge against Argüelles and had pressed governor Dulce to bring Argüelles to justice for the illegal disposition of the 100 missing bozales. Dulce had acceded to Zulueta's request and persuaded the U.S. Government to detain Argüelles, who was in the United States on business, and ship him to Cuba.

Alberto's classmates were almost evenly divided on Dulce's handling of the Argüelles case. Some lauded the governor for enforcing the anti-slave rule against his underling; others faulted him for acting unilaterally and causing the deportation of one who had not been tried, let alone convicted, of the alleged offenses. One of the most vociferous defenders of Dulce was Maximiliano Amondo, a relative of Zulueta on his mother's side. Maximiliano argued loudly: "Dulce did the right thing. Argüelles deserved to be punished for going after those importing Negro slaves. Cuba needs more slaves to support its industries. After all, those bozales are almost animals and putting them on the fields to cut cane is a better fate for them than living like savages in Africa."

Alberto thought of ignoring Maximiliano's diatribe, but his stomach turned at the depiction of Black captives as subhuman. Facing Maximiliano, who was taller than him by a couple of inches and a lot beefier, he responded: "You say that because Dulce is a stooge for your uncle Zulueta, who is well known as the biggest negrero in Cuba."

That might have ended the matter except that Maximiliano chose to respond scornfully: "Better a negrero than an ass-licking whore of Lincoln, as all you chickenhearted liberals are."

Alberto had rarely gotten into any fights growing up, but the fat bastard had gone beyond the limits of what one could tolerate. He lunged at Maximiliano, and both threw ineffectual punches at each other until a priest separated them.

Alberto got three things out of his fight with Maximiliano: a swollen eye, two days of detention, and a reputation as a liberal stalwart. The first two were gone in a few days; the third stayed with him through the rest of his stay in Guanabacoa and many years beyond.

Chapter 4

Pilón, June 5, 1864: Scandal

A lie has no leg, but a scandal has wings.
Thomas Fuller

*G*raciela **was not** a religious person and avoided going to church as much as possible. However, Ernestina's niece Teresita had been born in April and according to the Catholic Church doctrine, needed to be baptized without delay. Accordingly, her parents decided that the baby was strong enough to be baptized six weeks after birth. The ceremony was scheduled to take place on Sunday, June 5, the third Sunday after Pentecost, just before the Liturgy of the Word.

Being the principal mass of the week, virtually all of Pilón's faithful had gathered in the parish church for the Sunday service. Father Pastor, gray and bent under the weight of his almost seventy years, officiated. He performed the baptismal rite with dispatch and turned to the scheduled biblical reading. For that day, the reading was Matthew 10, in which Jesus instructs his twelve apostles to travel to the towns of Galilee and preach there. Father Pastor read verses 14-15: "If anyone will not welcome you or listen to your words, leave that home or town, and shake the dust off your feet. Truly I tell you, it will be more bearable for Sodom and Gomorrah on the day of judgment than for that town."

At the mention of Sodom and Gomorrah, a low whisper spread across the nave, and all eyes turned to the front row, where

Graciela and Ernestina sat, holding hands, next to the baby's parents. Father Pastor cleared his throat and began his homily, which centered on the need to carry God's message to all unbelievers. At one point, the Father likened those rejecting the word of Christ to the terrible sinners of Sodom and Gomorrah, equally deserving of eternal damnation. At those words, the earlier whispers became louder and the voice of one woman for some reason resonated clearly above the hubbub: "Yes, God will punish those tortilleras!"

The hubbub transformed into a wordless approving chorus, with all eyes now focused on the front row.

Father Pastor sought to calm the congregation: "Brothers, please be quiet. Respect the sanctity of this Holy Service." His plea failed to bring calm to the proceedings, and as loud whispering continued Graciela rose and, grabbing Ernestina's arm, walked the entire length of the church, opened the door, and strode resolutely into the early summer sunlight. Her face was rigid with anger as they sped away.

"I've to get out of this fucking town!" spat Graciela, as they sought the temporary shelter of Ernestina's home.

Chapter 5

La Habana, July 1864

*D*ear Mother:

I hope this letter finds you in fine health and good spirits.

I write to share some good news. Father Clappers, my advisor, met with me yesterday to let me know that, on account of my good progress in the preparation courses, he is willing to write a letter recommending my admission to the University of La Habana. I intend to file an application to the Law School with the aim of starting this September. God willing, if I am admitted and do well in my studies, I will graduate five years from now, in June 1869, as a member of the legal profession. Wish me luck.

Give a warm hug to my sisters, when you see them, and hello to Uncle Leonardo. Much love to you,

Your devoted son,
Alberto

Chapter 6

New York, October 27, 1864: Lost

*Sometimes gain comes from losing, and sometimes loss
comes from gaining.*
LaoTzu

Upon arriving in New York City by steamship, Graciela and several hundred immigrants and their baggage were loaded onto a barge and towed to the wharf at Battery Park on the south end of Manhattan. Beyond the wharf lay Castle Garden, a circular sandstone former fort that served as the immigration depot for the city of New York.

After a medical inspection, the immigrants were ushered into the fort and led to a huge space known as the rotunda. The immigrant registration depot was located at the center, surrounded by a vast waiting area. It included a quadrangle of desks for the processing of the passengers, as well as restrooms flanking the main entrance. The spacious interior was suitable for a stay of several hours, with vendors selling bread, cheese, and milk, and a kitchen for immigrants to cook for themselves. The depot lacked sleeping accommodations, but the fort was well heated during the cold months and could house roughly three thousand people overnight.

The new arrivals were separated into queues leading to registration desks staffed by clerks who spoke French and German; there was also one desk for those, like Graciela, who spoke some other language, or were fluent in English. At this desk, a clerk recorded Graciela's name, nationality, former place of residence, the name of the vessel on which she had arrived, the amount of money she had brought, and the names of any relatives already in the United States. While registration was in progress, porters unloaded the arriving passengers' luggage off the pier and brought it into a baggage room.

When Graciela's processing was completed, she proceeded to the baggage room to retrieve the large travel trunk that contained her clothes and other personal items. She went back and forth to the room for over an hour, searching for the trunk. It was not there.

***

Later, Graciela sat on a bench surrounded by strange looking, oddly dressed people milling about the main reception area. Her nostrils were assaulted by the pungent smells of salami, cooking meats, and body odors and her ears were pounded by the loud conversations and the screams of children and wailing babies. As she waited in that bizarre setting for word from the authorities on the search for her luggage, her mood darkened. She remembered her scornful reaction to her sister's elopement, a confirmation of Carmela's foolishness. Unlike her sister, Graciela thought of herself as a rational, calm person. And yet, she had allowed her distress to prompt a course of action that might prove as thoughtless as the actions she had condemned in her sibling. But no, her decision to leave Cuba was not the act of a rebellious teenager, but arose from the recognition that life for the likes of her would be burdensome at best, hazardous at worst. She lived in a Catholic-run, buttoned-down provincial backwater, where sexual deviation was abhorred almost as much as murder. Cosmopolitan New York City might be just as intolerant, but it was at least a bigger and better place to hide than Pilón.

She calmed down a bit. She was already resigned to the loss of her clothes, beauty products, everyday jewelry, poetry notebooks and sheet music ... all those things could be replaced over time, but would make a dent in the money her father had left in a trust account in New York for her to access when she was of age. She would have to visit with Mr. Theophilus Davis, the account's custodian, to make a first withdrawal. Luckily, when she boarded the barge to come ashore, she had kept in her possession the large travel bag in which she carried, besides grooming amenities, her best jewelry, money and identification documents, and her address book. She had written to Mr. Davis announcing her trip and the approximate date of her arrival, but wartime postal communications with the United States were unreliable and she had received no response from him. In any case, she would pay Mr. Davis a visit the following day.

Graciela was so immersed in planning on how to overcome her current predicament that she failed to notice the presence of someone in front of her. She was jolted out of her self-abstraction by a female voice:

"Excuse me, have you just arrived in this country?" It was the cultured voice of a lady who spoke loud and slowly, trying to make her words understood by foreign ears.

Graciela's command of English was good since her private tutor had taught her the essentials of the language. "Yes" she replied, startled.

"And where are you from, my dear?" Graciela was not sure she liked the untoward familiarity of the remark, but tried to reply politely: "I am from Cuba."

There was a surprising intake of breath as the lady repeated admiringly: "Cuba, Cuba. I have read a lot about Cuba in the papers, but never met anyone from there!"

Graciela raised her head and her eyes met the deep blue eyes of a very blond middle-aged woman dressed in a fur-lined violet pelisse and clothes that Graciela recognized as fashionable and expensive – just like the ones in her vanished trunk. No immigrant, she.

The women looked at each other intently. After a momentary pause, the lady proceeded with her questions:

"Have you come to New York to settle?"

The question stung, for Graciela was not sure of her ultimate plans, given that she had made none. She replied carefully: "I am not sure. I would like to see the city before deciding."

"Ah!" smiled the lady as she extended a hand in welcome that sported two rings: a diamond wedding ring and a gold ring holding a large red stone. "I'm Edith Farnsworth!" she declared cheerfully.

Graciela grasped the hand lightly and replied: "Me llamo Graciela Serrano."

"Pleased to meet you, Miss Serrano!" There was a slight emphasis on the "Miss," as if the lady was seeking reassurance. "Are you traveling by yourself?"

"Yes," Graciela answered, a touch too emphatically.

"Oh, the young are so brave these days!" exclaimed the lady. "I was born and raised here and have traveled a lot, but always accompanied by my parents at first, and now with Edward, my husband."

Graciela was not sure if the lady's declaration was meant as praise or implied criticism, so she remained silent. Mrs. Farnsworth went on: "So, what are your plans for your stay in New York?"

The stranger's question brought Graciela back to the reality of her situation. In a voice that was close to tears, she acknowledged: "I don't know! My luggage has been lost or stolen, so all I have are the clothes I am wearing!"

The lady sat next to Graciela and put a sympathetic hand on the young woman's shoulder. "Poor thing! It must be the work of those damned runners!"

"What do you mean by runners?" replied Graciela.

"There are bands of outlaws that roam around this port area looking for things to steal or smuggle" started Mrs. Farnsworth. "Irish, I bet," she ventured. "The Emigration Board and the city police have their hands full trying to keep them out, but sometimes they use kids to sneak into the baggage room and walk off with whatever they can snatch. It's disgusting!" She noticed the dismay her words were causing and quickly added: "but maybe your baggage has just been misplaced, and will eventually turn up!"

"I have been told to stay around this main room while they complete their search" noted Graciela.

"Oh, that's silly!" replied Mrs. Farnsworth airily. "A lady of quality like you shouldn't have to hang around this foreign riff-raff! I tell you what: come to my house with me. We'll have some tea and maybe a bite while we wait for the police to do their investigation. With luck, they will recover your baggage in no time!"

Graciela was startled at the offer. "I couldn't possibly …" she began. Mrs. Farnsworth interrupted: "It's no trouble. I live in Gramercy, not far from here. My carriage is waiting outside. We can be home in no time!"

Graciela was suspicious and afraid of being abducted. On the other hand, this lady did not look like a criminal, and her friendly air appeared to be genuine. "We would need to let the desk know we are leaving" she protested weakly.

"Don't worry. I'll take care of it" announced Mrs. Farnsworth and led Graciela back to the registration desk. Minutes later, they were installed in a Brougham carriage driven by a livered Black man whom Mrs. Fansworth addressed as Joshua. As the horse started its progress uptown, Graciela asked the question that had been floating in the back of her mind since the start of their encounter: "What were you doing at Castle Garden this afternoon? Were you expecting someone coming from abroad?"

"I have two daughters, five and seven years of age. I have been looking for a foreign immigrant to serve as an au pair to handle the care and education of my children. I have gone to the immigration center several times in search of such a person."

Chapter 7

New York, October 29, 1864: Found

*Perhaps the safest prediction we can make
about the future is that it will surprise us.*
George Leonard

Joshua **was instructed** to take Graciela to her meeting with Theophilus Davis and thereafter convey her to a boarding-house that Mrs. Farnsworth had selected. Although presumably a straightforward errand, Graciela's meeting with Mr. Davis turned out vastly different than she had anticipated. Mr. Davis was the head of the Continental Trust Company, located on Pine Street, in the heart of New York's financial district. Graciela had difficulty being received by him, for she was showing up unannounced and presenting a disreputable appearance by wearing the same wrinkled, soiled clothes she had on when she arrived in New York. After an argument with the receptionist in which Graciela waved at the woman's face the letter of introduction that had been issued by the U.S. consul in Santiago, she was finally ushered into a conference room and Mr. Davis joined her shortly thereafter.

Theophilus Davis was an elderly man with thinning white hair and a graying goatee to match. He appeared surprised at Graciela's unexpected visit and adopted the insincere smile of someone who was trying to get through a difficult meeting as quickly as possible.

"I remember your father well because he was one of my first clients when I started to work here in 1845. He was a very smart and charming man, and I liked him a lot. His wife had just given birth to their third child and he wanted to set up separate trusts for each of his children to protect them financially from the vagaries of business in Cuba. You and your sister are now over twenty-one years old and eligible to access your funds. Your brother will be able to do the same thing in a couple of years."

"That's good," said Graciela, "because I am thinking of moving to this country and will need funds to live on while I am getting settled."

"Good, good" replied Mr. Davis. "There is a small problem, though."

Graciela looked at the man with a start. "A problem?"

"Not with the trust itself" clarified Davis, "but with the assets in the trust."

"What do you mean??"

Davis issued a little cough. "Your father believed that cotton was a safe investment because no matter what happened people would always need clothes, so he had me put most of the money in each trust into buying stock of companies that invested heavily in Southern cotton plantations. However, after the start of the war, we quickly blockaded the South, cutting off any cotton trade. The stock of the companies in which we invested for your father's trusts is almost worthless now. It may bounce back once the war is over, but if we were to liquidate it now, you would get almost nothing."

"Do you mean to tell me that I cannot touch my trust until after the North wins the war, if that ever happens?!"

"Patience, my dear. Only a few days ago Sheridan won a major victory in the Shenandoah Valley. The war should be over soon…"

"In the meantime, what am I going to do?!"

"There is some cash in your trust that I could disburse if you want it."

"How much?"

"I think about twenty dollars or so, I would have to run the numbers."

"That wouldn't even cover the cost of my return trip to Cuba!"

"I am very sorry. It is this blasted war that is messing everything up. Do you want me to get you that cash anyway?"

Graciela swallowed hard to repress her tears. "Yes, please."

"You caught me unprepared, since I was unaware of your coming. Please come back tomorrow afternoon."

***

When Joshua took Graciela to the boardinghouse and she checked into her room, Graciela exploded into long-suppressed tears. She had never felt so lonely and abandoned. What was she going to do?

It was dinnertime but she was not hungry, and she expected the food at the cheap boardinghouse would be lousy. She threw herself on the bed, still fully dressed, and tried to get some relief from sleep.

She was awakened by a knock. She ignored it, but the knocking persisted, so she shambled to the front door and opened it. It was one of the maids.

"Miss, there is someone downstairs looking for you."

"For me? I know no one in this town."

"It's a Negro. A coachman, I think."

"Please let him in. I will be down shortly."

"I am sorry, miss. This is a Christian establishment. Negroes are not allowed."

Graciela frowned with disgust. "Fine, I will come down in a few minutes."

***

Graciela was not surprised when she saw the visitor. It was

Joshua. He greeted her with a smile and bowed. "Good evening again, Miss Serrano. I have good news."

"What is it, Joshua? I really could use some good news."

"Your trunk was found and was delivered to Mrs. Farnsworth's residence."

It was good news, but not enough to make up for the disaster her life had become.

"Oh, thank you. Did you bring it with you?"

"No, miss. Mrs. Farnsworth asked me to fetch you and bring you to her house to check the contents of the trunk in case she needs to report to the police that something is missing."

That is strange, thought Graciela. Fine. I have nothing better to do. "Will you bring me back here afterwards?"

"Of course."

"Let's go, then."

***

As they entered the brownstone, Joshua led Graciela past the parlor and two other rooms and into a lavishly appointed dining room, where a linen, gold-ornament tablecloth covered a large table. The entire Farnsworth family was sitting around the table, waiting for food to be served.

"Oh, hello, Graciela" greeted Mrs. Farnsworth. "Let me introduce you: the gentleman at the head of the table is my husband, Edward." Mrs. Farnsworth pointed to a dour looking man wearing a business suit, who nodded gravely. "And these are my darlings, Jane and Anne" she said, identifying two plain girls who curtsied in greeting.

Mrs. Farnsworth went on breezily: "Please take a seat next to me. You are right in time for supper."

"But… I am not dressed for dinner… and don't want to impose on …"

"Don't be silly. You are not imposing. In fact, you'll help us make decisions."

"Decisions?"

"Yes. In a few weeks we will be hosting a Thanksgiving din-

100

ner for six of the leading families in town. Eliza here is trying some potential new dishes." As if on cue, two Black servants came in through the back door: an aging male in uniform and a plump elderly female wearing an apron over her dress.

"Virgil, please start with some Sauvignon Blanc for everyone…" started Mrs. Farnsworth, who interrupted herself to ask: "Do you drink wine, Graciela?" As Graciela nodded in the affirmative, the lady continued: "and apple juice for the girls."

"Yes, ma'am" replied Virgil. As he poured the wine into blown crystal white wine glasses, Eliza began setting appetizers on the table: blue point oysters, quenelles, olives stuffed with pimento or gorgonzola cheese, turtle soup. When both servants left the room, Graciela whispered: "Are they slaves?"

Mrs. Farnsworth uttered a scornful little laugh. "No, my dear. Slavery was outlawed in New York forty years ago. They just came with the house when we bought it." Graciela was secretly relieved, since she was White in appearance (save for her kinky hair) but was actually carrying Negro blood from her paternal grandfather Lázaro, who was of mixed race.

After the appetizers came the entrees: prime rib with Yorkshire pudding, roasted goose with onions and squash, a firm white fish that Graciela did not recognize, and roast turkey, all accompanied by over half a dozen vegetables, some of which – like sweet potatoes – were similar, but not quite the same, as the Cuban root vegetables she knew. Virgil poured Côte de Nuits burgundy throughout the dinner, which ended with a salad course – which Graciela did not touch, as she was already too full – followed by a dazzling array of desserts: English trifle, petit fours, plum pudding with maple brandy sauce, mince, apple and pumpkin pie, and almond cake with maple frosting.

Eliza and Virgil cleared the table and brought coffee, sweet cider, and assorted cheeses and nuts, and retreated, presumably to do the dishes. Mrs. Farnsworth turned to Graciela amiably: "Did you enjoy your dinner, dear?"

Graciela had consumed a lot of food and drunk several glasses of wine; the outstanding dinner had managed to temporarily blot her predicament out of her mind. Now, the reality of her situation came back to her. She started: "Yes, many thanks," and then broke into a disconsolate cry.

"What's the matter?" asked Mrs. Farnsworth solicitously.

"I am in a terrible bind" blurted out Graciela. "I came to New York to collect moneys that had been placed in trust for me by my late father. As it turns out, the money is all tied up in cotton-backed securities that are currently worthless." She stopped to catch her breath and then resumed her sobbing.

"Fear not, darling" consoled Mrs. Farnsworth. "The war will soon be over and things will go back to normal." From the head of the table came the voice of Edward Farnsworth, who had remained silent through most of the dinner: "I would not count on the cotton trade ever recovering. England and France have now adapted to the absence of cotton from the Confederate states and are getting their supply from Egypt and India and even Brazil."

At those words, Graciela started to cry even more loudly than before. "I am ruined!" she wailed.

Mrs. Farnsworth tightened her grip on Graciela's heaving shoulders. "Well, dear, all is not lost. I have an idea!"

"An idea?"

"Yes. I mentioned to you yesterday that I am looking for a governess for my daughters, since I had to fire a very lazy girl who was working for us in that capacity. Why don't you come work for us? I can't pay you much, but you will have room and board and a small salary to tide you over until your finances improve."

Graciela's instinct, as well as her pride, counseled immediately against the surprising offer. On the other hand, she was in desperate straits: stranded in a foreign land, penniless, and away from everyone she knew. Alcohol and desperation were a powerful combination: she took a deep breath. "You are too kind. I accept your offer."

"Great" replied Mrs. Farnsworth with an air of satisfaction. "I will have Joshua take you back to the boarding house to gather your belongings. In the meantime, Agnes will set up a room for you."

As they got up and Mrs. Farnsworth escorted Graciela back to the parlor, the lady noted cheerfully: "Isn't it convenient that your big trunk is already here?"

Chapter 8

Yara, November 1864: An Unexpected Encounter

*I think it surprises a lot of people thatI'm still around, you know,
still – that I'm not pushing up daisies, as they say.*
James Taylor

Rodolfo **was awakened** from his uneasy sleep by the furious barking of both of his dogs. He reckoned that the noise was caused by the scent of some wild animal that had caught the attention of Pipo and Chicho. He tossed in his cot, ready to try to fall asleep again. However, the dogs' commotion was followed by a sudden banging on the door of the house. Rodolfo sat up, brushing sleep from his eyes, and was getting his pants on when there was a loud crash and the sound of cracked wood: someone was forcing his way into his house.

His pants still unbuttoned and shirtless, Rodolfo ran to the cottage's main room and seized his shotgun just as five men entered the dwelling: Black men dressed in rags and armed with guns, staves, and machetes. Rodolfo immediately realized what they were: bandits, probably escaped slaves from some palenque in the mountains.

Rodolfo was in a dark mood and did not much care whether he lived or died. He raised his shotgun and waved it left and right at the interlopers. "Cabrones, you picked the wrong place to steal from!" To his astonishment, the leader of the pack replied in a voice he immediately recognized: "Hola, Ro!"

Rodolfo lowered the gun as the man came forward and embraced him. "Rino? Is that you?"

The man before him bore only scant resemblance to his baby brother. He seemed to have grown a couple of head lengths, his body had bulked up considerably and appeared to have lost all vestiges of fat. Only his fierce eyes betrayed the kid who had been his companion for all but the last five years.

"I thought you were dead! I kept looking for you after … what you did, and found no trace of you. You had just disappeared!"

"You were not the only one chasing after me. Groups of bounty hunters were combing through the mountains trying to get me. I barely escaped capture a couple of times and kept running east, almost to the coast. I ended up near an old Indian town by a village called Yateras and joined a palenque of escaped slaves, who took me in and made me one of their own. Life has been getting harder for us in the last year from being chased by the law, so we moved our operations west and ended up in the mountains south of Guisa near here. Tonight, I decided to drop by and scare Manuel for old times' sake. But how about you? How come you are still here? And where are the Galáns?"

"Manuel Galán has been dead for years, and Isabel has moved to Bayamo. I now run the place. The families that work for me in the coffee business live in the bohíos behind the house. But I live alone."

"No sweeties to keep you warm?"

"A few months after you left town, I did get married to Carmela and we moved here together…"

"So, you finally nailed her!" exclaimed Rino, his bearded face opening into a wolfish grin.

"Yeah. It's a long story. She became my wife and we had two kids, but a year ago she left me and went back to her mother in Pilón, taking the children with her."

"And you let her do that?" Rino's expression turned incredulous and then threatening, reminding Rodolfo of his brother's explosive temper.

"I love her, and love the kids even more. I've been trying to convince her to come back to me but, so far, she has resisted and I don't want to try to force her."

"It looks like I need to pay a visit to Pilón sometime soon" offered the bandit.

"Please don't. Your shooting of Leonardo Serrano is still the talk of that town. They would kill you on sight if you were seen there."

"I don't think that would be so easy for them to do. Anyhow, the bastard deserved what he got." Rino ran his fingers over the scars that showed on the portion of his face that was not covered by the beard.

"Stop that," chided Rodolfo. "He surely is paying for what he did."

Rino gave a start, his eyes widening with surprise. "You mean he is still alive?"

"Barely. He's paralyzed and spends all the time in bed."

"But I didn't manage to kill him!"

"No."

"As I said, it's time for me to make a trip to Pilón."

Chapter 9

Pilón, December 1864: Upheavals

Your present circumstances don't determine where you can go.
They merely determine where you start.
Nido Qubein

The year's holidays proved to be a trying time for the Serrano family. A week before Christmas, Leonardo suffered a stroke and died two days later. Among the condolence calls that Cecilia received, the most stressful one came from Mateo Ruiz, Leonardo's right-hand man for the last ten years. He seemed genuinely stricken at his boss' passing, and was also bearing some difficult news.

"Doña Cecilia, it pains me to have to tell you this, but I have been diagnosed as having contracted tuberculosis, probably from contact with the Chinese workers we imported to work at the sugar mill. My doctor insists that my survival from this deadly disease requires my moving into an outdoor environment with access to fresh air, ample sunlight, and moderate temperatures. My daughter, who lives in Trinidad, has found a cottage for me and my wife in the mountains not far from her own home. We have decided to move there, and intend to do so before Easter. Therefore, I must resign my position at *Santa Cruz* effective as of the end of January. I will assist you the best I can to find a replacement for me during the next month so that there can be an orderly transition of my duties."

"Can't you find a similar environment near here?" asked Cecilia.

"It is too warm and too close to the Caribbean. At any rate, my treatment requires rest and relaxation, and those would be impossible for me while retaining my current duties at the mill. I am terribly sorry to inflict my health issues on you at this difficult time, but my wife is also in a delicate condition and I must try to get well, not just for my own sake, but primarily for hers."

***

"What are we going to do?" asked Carmela, wringing her hands.

"I will contact our agents again to see if we can sell this damned business. I really want to get back to La Habana."

Chapter 10

Pilón, February 1865: Farewell

Any change, even a change for the better,
is always accompanied by discomforts.
Arnold Bennett

*J*anuary came and went, and at the end of the month Mateo Ruiz departed. His offer to train a successor went unfulfilled, for no suitable candidates to replace him had been found.

The week of his departure, Mateo met with his bosses – Cecilia and Carmela – to render a final account of the status of operations at *Santa Cruz*. He was apologetic, but his report reflected the arduous effort he had undertaken despite his failing health.

"As you know, the zafra that is underway will continue until the rainy season starts around May. This is the busiest time of the year because the cane is ripening and must be harvested and processed within thirty-six hours, then boiled and reduced to crystalline form. I have endeavored to assemble and organize the work force on the cane fields the best I could and developed a transportation schedule to deliver the cane to the mill. However, now that importation of additional slaves into the island is prohibited, we have had to make do with the available slave population, supplemented by contract Chinese workers and temporary hands from Haiti and Jamaica. I managed to get it done for this year, but strongly recommend that the manpower search start earlier next year because, as slaves become emancipated, they seek easier work elsewhere than in the fields."

"Now, much needs to be done at each of the three main buildings of the mill: the milling house, where cane is squeezed to collect the juice; the boiling house, where the juice is clarified, filtered, and concentrated; and the purging or curing house, where the juice is exposed to air and sun to dry thoroughly and turn into sugar grains. Some repairs need to be made to the existing machinery, and the mill engineer needs to see that those are carried out; I left him a list."

"Most importantly, however, we need to make continuous upgrades and improvements to the machinery that we have installed to reduce production costs. The sugar market is very competitive and the only way we can stay in business, as Don Leonardo used to say, is to produce more sugar, faster and cheaper."

"Ay, Mateo, how are we going to manage without you?" lamented Cecilia.

"Dios dará," replied Mateo.

Chapter 11

Pilón, February 1865: La Traviata

Every parent is at some time the father of the unreturned prodigal,
with nothing to do but keep his house open to hope.
John Ciardi

*I*t **had been** four months since Cecilia received a cryptic, two paragraph letter from Graciela announcing that she was tired of living in Cuba and was moving to the United States, a "more civilized country." The letter indicated she would be sending a follow-up letter with the new address, but no such letter had yet arrived.

Cecilia was increasingly worried about the safety of her rebellious daughter, but concerns over the running of the mill without the benefit of a guiding male occupied her thoughts leaving little time to think about Graciela, whose scandalous behavior had filled the family with shame. It was only on February 2, the day of La Candelaria (Candlemas), that the fate of her daughter re-emerged to the surface of Cecilia's mind. It happened during the traditional procession that paraded the images of Virgin Mary and Baby Jesus around the streets of Pilón, to be followed by the blessing of the spring candles at the church. During the procession, Cecilia caught sight of Ernestina Cueto, who was seldom seen out in public after the commotion at the church half a year earlier. Her first impulse was to approach Ernestina to ask whether she had received any news from Graciela, but she restrained herself. She would not be seen in public talking to that descarada!

Later on, after going back to the manor house, Cecilia was overcome by guilt and took off on foot to the small house on the outskirts of town where Ernestina lived, alone with her cats.

The meeting of the two women was tense, and was almost aborted when Ernestina started to slam the door after realizing who was paying her a call. Only the anxious outcry from Cecilia made her stop halfway and ask in a biting tone: "What do you want?"

Cecilia could only let out five words: "Have you heard from Graciela?" Then she began to cry loudly.

Ernestina opened the door wide: "Come in!"

The two women sat across from each other in the living room, not saying anything at first. "You have not heard from Graciela either?" Ernestina started.

"No!" replied Cecilia, almost shouting. "She had a short letter hand-delivered to our home announcing her departure for the United States. Nothing else since."

"After the incident at the bautizo of my niece, your daughter and I began quarrelling nonstop. I tried to convince her to ignore the reaction of the people of this town, but she was angry beyond reason. She kept saying that our life would be miserable as long as we stayed in Pilón and when I countered with an offer to move elsewhere, she would respond that anywhere we went in Cuba it would be the same thing. She finally brought up the money she had in trust in the United States and suggested that we go there together. I told her I had a big family and was unwilling to move abroad, particularly since I don't know English and don't like the Yankees. So, one day she announced, out of the blue, that she had booked passage on a steamship bound for New York City and was leaving for Santiago in two days. I pleaded with her to stay, pointed out all the risks of going to a country in the middle of a civil war, and appealed to her love for me and for her family. All in vain."

Ernestina stopped for a moment to catch her breath, and Cecilia replied apologetically: "I am sorry. My daughter is vain and obstinate. It was wrong for her to treat you that way. She did the same thing to us."

Ernestina then asked: "Have you tried to contact the bank in New York where she said she had all that money?"

Cecilia shook her head. "I have been too tied up with other things. I will write them immediately. I wish there was a faster way to contact people abroad!"

"Well, if you find anything will you let me know? I'll do the same." And then, almost as an afterthought, she added: "I still love her, you know!"

The two women embraced.

Chapter 12

La Habana, February 27, 1865: Smiling Irish Eyes

Do you think anybody knows that I'm Irish?
Niall Horan

*T*he University of La Habana, one of the first in the New World, opened in 1728 in a sixteenth century ecclesiastical property that had initially been the Church of Nuestra Señora de Santa María de la Consolación and later San Juan de Letrán. The campus was located at the north end of the oldest section of the city, adjacent to the Palace of the Captain Generals of Cuba, and within view of the entrance of the harbor. Originally run as a Catholic school by the Dominican Fathers, the university became a secular institution in 1842 when the order was temporarily banished by the Spanish government.

Despite the change in its management, the university had retained its conservative bent, being supported by the colonial elite. Learning was confined to private tutoring (for affluent families) and a higher education curriculum that included Art and Philosophy, Theology, Science, Law and Medicine, dispensed by teachers often selected through patronage instead of merit.

By 1865, the university's student population included both criollos and peninsulares. As was to be expected by people whose relatives occupied all the levels of political power in Cuba, the peninsulares were unanimous in their opposition to any economic or political change to the authoritarian regime that ruled Cuba, especially if it affected their families' interests. The criollos, on the other hand, were split into three factions: the reformistas, who sought no drastic change in Spanish rule but advocated increased political autonomy for Cuba and lightening of the oppressive colonial economic measures; the anexionistas, an increasingly marginalized group who favored Cuba's becoming part of the United States despite the civil war that continued to rage in that country; and the independistas, a small but growing minority that advocated Cuba's complete independence.

Alberto's political sensitivities had sharpened during his months at the Escuelas Pías. He had enrolled in the Law school, joining Carlos Masó, now in his third year in the Medicine school. Alberto and Carlos lived in the same boardinghouse and together attended the social and cultural events in the city and the political events at the university. Both were reformistas, but their political activities were limited to attending the periodic reformist gatherings.

Those gatherings were mainly held indoors, but on that cold February morning the reformistas and independistas were rallying on the square outside the university to celebrate the anniversary of the Dominican Republic's declaration of independence from Haiti in 1844. This was a sensitive topic, for Spain had reoccupied the Dominican Republic in 1861 and was still fighting a losing war against the Dominican insurgents.

The rally attendees shouted slogans like "Freedom for the Dominican people!" "Spain out of Santo Domingo!" and "Stop the carnage!"

As the speakers and other participants voiced their opposition to the war effort, a dozen peninsulares, some too old to be students, entered the square from the waterfront side of O'Reilly Street, carrying cudgels and other improvised weapons. They shouted angry insults:

"Traitors! Maricones!"

A fight immediately broke out between the two groups. Alberto tried to get out of the way but as he was doing so, he collided with a young girl who was facing defiantly the peninsulares, shouting back at them: "Bandits!" "Cowards!"

Alberto and the girl lost balance and fell to the ground in a heap. One of the peninsulares, armed with a club, approached running and raised the club intending to strike the girl. Alberto, noticing the blow coming, jumped protectively to shelter her and took the blow on the right shoulder.

He got up slowly, wincing from the excruciating pain. The attacker was getting ready to inflict another blow when he was jumped on by Carlos and another student, who struck and kicked him repeatedly. A scuffle ensued, interrupted after a few minutes by the sound of whistles and the arrival on the scene of a contingent of the recently established city police force. Fighters on both sides dispersed quickly, with Carlos leading Alberto and the girl to safety on the threshold of a nearby building.

The girl, who had not spoken since the peninsular's attack, turned to Alberto, who was moaning. "Are you in pain? Thanks for protecting me from that brute!"

Alberto looked at the girl for the first time. She was very white in complexion, with deep green eyes and kinky ginger hair that sparkled in the sunshine. She wore a simple open neck blouse with short sleeves and a knee length dark green dress that almost matched the color of her eyes. She was strikingly odd and pretty in a very foreign way. "It was nothing" he forced himself to say, blinking from the pain.

"You are a poor liar" she replied brightly. "Happy to meet you. I'm Irene Cowan."

Chapter 13

Pilón, March 15, 1865: A Savior Arrives

*When you go looking for rescue, you end up
trapped in your own weakness.*
Deb Caletti

*I*llustrious Mrs. Serrano:

I have become aware of the difficulties you are encountering in filling the position of administrator of the Santa Cruz facility after the resignation of Mateo Ruiz. I take the liberty of writing to introduce for your thoughtful consideration Mr. Faustino Rocha, an experienced sugar mill executive, as a potential replacement for Mr. Ruiz.

I have known Mr. Rocha for over ten years; our firm was counsel to the owners of the Las Maracas sugar mill, located in the Valle de los Ingenios near Trinidad. Las Maracas closed down six months ago because the owners filed for bankruptcy and Mr. Rocha has been searching for suitable employment since that time. I believe him to be extremely capable and knowledgeable of sugar production matters and perhaps he would be a suitable administrator for Santa Cruz. While I recommend him for that position, I leave the ultimate decision in your capable hands.

I take this opportunity to reiterate my highest consideration and esteem.

Respectfully yours,
Isidro Álvarez, Esq.

Carmela read the letter twice, using the time to reflect on its contents and the opportunity it raised for straightening out the mill's affairs. The letter had been hand-delivered by Mr. Rocha himself, who had stated at the onset of his unannounced visit that he regarded this matter to be of utmost personal and professional importance and was unwilling to trust its deliverance to the vagaries of the mail system. The man sat on an armchair across from the divan where Carmela sat, fiddling nervously with the porcelain cup holding the coffee that his hostess had offered.

"Mr. Rocha, I am impressed by the strong recommendation from this Mr. Álvarez but we don't know him and must learn more about you before deciding. Please tell me about yourself and your credentials."

"Madame, I have prepared a written summary of my work history, which I am happy to submit for your perusal." Rocha extracted a folded piece of paper from the inside pocket of his suit and handed it over to Carmela. "Please take your time to review it. I will be happy to answer any questions."

Carmela glanced quickly at the handwritten document and set it aside. "I will show this to my mother and we will get back to you if it raises any specific issues. Right now, just tell me about yourself."

Rocha shrugged his shoulders deprecatingly. "There is not that much to say. I was born and raised in Cienfuegos. My parents were poor, but they sacrificed to get me an education and, later, an apprenticeship as a mechanic at *Las Maracas*. My employment at that mill is the only job I ever held, though in the course of over thirty years I have gone through every position, getting more responsibility each time. I am single, a devout Catholic, and a loyal subject of her Majesty Queen Isabel. I only drink on holidays, don't smoke or use opium, and don't do bolita or gamble on fighting roosters. I am boring but honest."

Carmela's lips parted in a brief smile. "I need to think about your application and discuss it with my mother, who is gone to Manzanillo shopping with the children, but she will be back tomorrow. Where are you staying?"

"They rent rooms at a local bar, *El Malecón*. Are you familiar with it?"

The smile disappeared from Carmela's face, to be replaced by a frown. "Yes, I am."

***

Two days later, Faustino Rocha returned to the *Santa Cruz* manor house and was received by Cecilia, fresh from her morning beauty treatment. After exchanging greetings, Rocha remarked admiringly: "Madam, if I may be allowed a brazen remark, your already attractive face shines with a supernatural splendor. If I may inquire, what magic do you employ to further enhance what would appear unsurpassable?"

Cecilia's face reddened slightly but she hastened to reply: "Mr. Rocha, thank you for the compliment, but a woman in her fifties like me would require more than magic to recover the freshness of youth. If you must know, I apply a cold cream made from almond oil and rosewater to moisturize my skin and a lemon juice toner to brighten my complexion."

"Madam, please call me Faustino. I refuse to believe you are in your fifties. I would not have guessed a day older than thirty-five."

"Oh, Faustino, you flatter me too much. Let's move to business. I have read your letter of recommendation and received a favorable report from my daughter Carmela. Now I would like for you to go into more detail about your experience…"

Rocha interrupted her. "Yes, madam, I would be happy to do that, but first let me relate to you my first impressions of your facility."

"What do you mean first impressions?"

"Yesterday being Sunday, I felt it would be inappropriate for me to disturb you on the Lord's Day, so instead I conducted an impromptu tour of *Santa Cruz*. My first observation is that physical security at your mill is rather lax. I was able to enter the premises unchallenged and walk back and forth into and around all the main buildings without meeting a guard. I strongly urge that you hire well trained guards to protect your valuable assets from pilferage and theft."

"Thanks, Faustino. Duly noted."

"I can recommend a company that can be retained to provide those services. Anyway, my overall inspection revealed no major deficiencies that could interfere with the completion of the current zafra, but there are certain actions that must be accomplished during the tiempo muerto to guarantee that, come January, the next zafra will be a success."

"Your predecessor left us with a list of required actions. I would like to compare that list with your observations."

"I would be happy to do so, although I hear that Mr. Ruiz was a thorough and capable man and doubt that he left out anything important. Of course, new matters may have arisen in the last couple of months."

"Well, Faustino, it is getting to be mid-morning. Let's cut this meeting short. When can you start working for us?"

"Tomorrow, if you would want me to."

"The administrator's house has been vacant for well over a month. I will have the place cleaned and aired, furniture replaced as needed, and linens and other household items brought in. Why don't you come in tomorrow so I can introduce you to the staff so that you can start work on Wednesday?"

"Thank you, madam. I will be here tomorrow, bright and

early."

"Not too early, please. How about nine-thirty?"

"Your wish is my command, madam. And eternal thanks for your confidence."

Later, Cecilia summarized to Carmela her conversation with Faustino Rocha, and concluded: "A charming and respectful man. I have the feeling he will be perfect for the job."

Carmela was not as enthusiastic as her mother, but nodded in agreement.

Chapter 14

La Habana, April 1865: A Picnic

Love makes your soul crawl out from its hiding place.
Zora Neale Hurston

*I*t was evident from the start that Alberto and Irene were a good match. He was unusually calm and collected for a Cuban and sought to dominate discourse only through the sharpness of his mind. Irene, by contrast, was a firebrand who unleashed the force of her opinions on her audience. They started sparring about everything from the moment Alberto had recovered enough from the blow received from the peninsular to be able to hold a sustained conversation.

A typical argument, which would be repeated countless times thereafter, was about politics. While both were nominally reformists, he advocated the pursuit of reforms in Spain's rule over Cuba, believing that the island's progress would best be furthered by remaining under the tutelage of the mother country; Irene grudgingly accepted reformism as a tactical step that would enable the Cuban population to better prepare for the unequal battle against the large occupying Spanish forces that had concentrated on the island after Spain lost most of the rest of its possessions in the New World.

"Why are you so opposed to the Spanish rule?" he would ask. "Is it because you are a foreigner from a different culture?"

Irene would react violently to any notion that she was less Cuban than Alberto. "My parents came to Cuba from Barbados, where they were indentured servants to a family of English colonists. They had secured overseas passage from England, receiving food, clothing, shelter, and a miserable salary in exchange for their labor. They were essentially White slaves. When the indenture period was over, they came to Oriente, where I was born eighteen years ago. The family ultimately moved to La Habana and my father opened a modest shoe repair business. Embracing our Irish heritage, my parents hated the English as hypocritical tyrants. I inherited from them the disdain for Old World rulers, except that the Spaniards in Cuba are rougher and more stupid than the English were. That's why I want them thrown out of Cuba."

Despite their differences, Alberto and Irene spent an increasing amount of time together. Irene did not attend the University: the idea of a woman getting a college degree and becoming a professional was unheard of; outside private tutoring, women's education was limited to household management and religious values. However, she had been taught at home and achieved a basic level of learning, which Alberto sought to expand by making her more aware of the arts, such as theater and music. Over the next six months, he took her frequently to the Teatro Tacón (one of the largest and most elegant performing centers in the Americas) to watch plays, Italian operas by Bellini and Donizetti, Spanish zarzuelas, and even Cuban-flavored musical compositions by Louis Moreau Gottschalk and others. Irene was not enthusiastic about Alberto's attempts to inflict culture on her, but appreciated his efforts.

One weekend in mid-April Alberto hired a carriage to take them to one of the parks in the suburb of El Cerro, which had been developed to the southwest of the bay as a summer resort with villas and country houses for the wealthy. It was not yet summer, so the park was empty. Alberto had packed a basket with freshly baked bread, cold cuts (chorizo, morcilla, tasajo), olives, pastelitos de guayaba, and a bottle of Rioja. They found a ledge from which there was a breathtaking view of the city, and sat down in a grassy area under an ancient flame tree. All was silent around them.

They ate and drank and chatted amiably until all the wine was consumed, and then drifted into a contented torpor. As the sun began to sink behind the city, Alberto shook himself from the lethargy and put his arms around Irene's waist. In a slurred voice he declared: "My dear, I think I am falling in love with you."

Irene's voice was also wobbly, but tinged with irony: "And what do you propose to do about it? Tell me…"

Alberto gulped to clear the lump on his throat, bent over, and replied to her challenge with a kiss that silenced her. And their lips were joined in what, in his later recollection, lasted an eternity.

Chapter 15

New York, April 1865: Stranger in a Strange Land

I used to think the worst thing in life was to end up
all alone. It's not. The worst thing in life is to end
up with people that make you feel all alone.
Robin Williams

Nearly **six months** had gone by since Graciela found herself marooned in New York City with no means of returning to Cuba or improving her situation. She had written twice to her mother in Pilón and once to Alberto in La Habana, but had received no response.

Graciela was skeptical of getting much help from the Spanish government; in her experience, Cuban-born nationals were at best second-class citizens, only a notch or two above slaves. Nonetheless, given her predicament she could not afford to ignore a potential source of assistance.

Thus, she travelled uptown to the Spanish Consulate, a non-descript narrow building with only a bronze plaque to serve as means of identification. She found the offices empty except for two clerks, one of which – a lady of dour countenance – delivered unhelpful news.

"Spain, like the other European powers save Russia, has declared her neutrality in the ongoing war between the States. We have been accused, however, of favoring the Confederacy because their stance, like ours, is in favor of slavery, and thus threats have been leveled against our diplomats. For that reason, the Queen has ordered most of our consulates in this country to be closed with only the embassy in Washington to remain in operation. Here in New York, we attend to the such consular business as is minimally required, considering that there is currently virtually no travel between Spain and the United States."

"Do you mean you cannot assist me, a Spanish national from her Cuban colony, to return to my homeland?"

"I am sorry, Miss, but we have no authority to spend the funds that would be required to transport you back to Cuba. As you know, our country's economic situation is difficult and the Cortes have decreed that only those Spanish citizens on official travel abroad can be given economic assistance in case of need."

Graciela's vision became blurred by tears, but she gritted her teeth and asked: "Can you at least see to it that a letter of mine to my relatives in Cuba is safely delivered? I have written them twice but, with the current state of communications, I have no way to know whether my letters have reached them."

The clerk's visage softened a bit and she declared: "Well, I can have your letter sent to the Embassy with a note that it be put in the diplomatic pouch that goes to Madrid, and from there to Cuba. It is a circuitous route, but your letter may eventually reach your relatives in Cuba."

Graciela sighed, and tears began flowing unbidden. "Could you please lend me some pen and paper and an envelope? I came from some distance away and don't have anything like that with me."

"Sure. Just one moment."

***

The only other institutional source of support that Graciela could think of was the Catholic Church. She was a non-believer, but was accustomed to the power wielded by the church in Cuba and hoped the similar influence could be exerted overseas by the American Church. She went to St. Joseph's Parish church in Greenwich Village, an institution well-known for supporting the growing Irish-Catholic population in Lower Manhattan and providing outreach – even a soup kitchen – to its parishioners. Entering past Hellenistic columns that supported the entrance, she walked into the nave and stopped, unsure of how to proceed, after walking a couple of steps into the darkened enclosure. It was a weekday mid-morning and the church was nearly empty. She was having second thoughts and debating whether to go away when a door creaked open in a booth to the left side of the nave and a bearded priest dressed in the black and white robes of the Dominican Order approached her.

"Greetings, my daughter. I'm Friar Bernard. How can I assist you? Do you wish to have your confession heard?"

Graciela relaxed a little. Dominican priests had been present in Cuba since the early days of the colony. "Good morning, Father" she replied. "I am a sinner, but I have come in need of temporal, not spiritual, help."

Friar Bernard frowned but motioned her to follow him. "Let's go to the sacristy. There we can talk privately."

They proceeded through a door to the side of the main altar and entered a room where the sacred vessels, vestments, and other articles needed for liturgical use were kept. They sat across from each other on velvet-covered chairs. "What is your need, my child?"

The dikes opened and Graciela described her predicament in a stream of words punctuated by loud intakes of breath. At the end, Friar Bernard asked softly: "What you have encountered is a terrible misfortune. But how can we help? Do you need food, or a place to stay? We help run a shelter for indigents not far from here, but I am not sure it is a place you would want to find yourself."

Graciela responded quickly. "No, Father; thanks. However, I know the Dominican Order has chapters all over the world. What I need is help letting my family know of my situation. Would it be possible for you to deliver a message to them through your churches in Cuba?"

Friar Bernard shook his head. "Our order was expelled from Spain and its colonies in 1837 but we have been partially reinstated. We do not have our own means of communication, but must depend on the regular mail like everyone else. I can look up our directory of churches in Cuba and write directly to the parish priest of one or more of them enclosing a letter of yours and asking that it be delivered to your family. Do you want me to do that?"

"It would be wonderful."

"Alright. Let's have you write identical letters and I will mail them separately to each of the churches still being run by Dominicans in Cuba. But you must understand that there are no assurances that any of the letters will find its destination."

"I understand, Father. But nothing is lost by trying."

"Alright. Let us do it, and keep our faith in God's providence."

Chapter 16

La Habana, May 1865: Hopes

> *Don't spend time beating on a wall,*
> *hoping to transform it into a door.*
> Coco Chanel

Alberto was spending a quiet evening with Irene when their enjoyment was interrupted by an insistent pounding on the locked door of Alberto's room. It was Carlos Masó, twitching with excitement: "You two, stop your carousing, you have to come with me right now!!"

Alberto, halfway between irritation and curiosity, flung his arm over his friend's shoulder to steady him and challenged: "Steady, Carlitos, calm down! Where is the fire?"

Carlos subsided a bit and explained: "There is a huge gathering starting now at the offices of El Siglo. El Partido Reformista is meeting to develop a list of demands to submit to the government in Madrid to see if we finally get some action on all the problems that we Cubans have been complaining about for years…"

Irene cut him off acidly: "You almost brought the door down for THAT? Do you really think those bastards in Spain are going to pay any attention to our complaints? Every time we squeak, they twist the noose harder."

"No, it is going to be different this time. A month ago, Francisco Serrano, the former Capitán General, gave two speeches in the Cortes asserting that it is imperative and urgent to institute political and administrative reforms in Cuba including restauration of Cuba's right to be represented in Parliament. Those in government appear to be receptive to Serrano's arguments. This is our opportunity to make our demands known!"

Alberto did not want to deflate his friend's enthusiasm so he decided to go along. He had no political experience, but had gone to a few meetings of the Reformist Party and had found its members to be too divided in ideology and objectives to be effective. Irene was even more skeptical: on the way to the meeting, she kept repeating: "this will be a waste of time."

It took several meetings besides the one they attended and a lot of heated exchanges, but eventually the Party came up with a declaration, the Manifesto of the Reformist Party, that set forth the changes the reformers demanded that the Spanish government implement: equal rights for Cubans and Spaniards on the island; Cuban representation in Parliament; limitations on the powers of the Capitanes Generales; greater political freedom; trade freedom and reduction of taxes; and the end of the slave trade. The demands contained in this declaration were intended to be formally submitted to the Spanish government later that year.

Throughout the process, Irene and, to a lesser degree, Alberto remained skeptical of the chances of success of the Cubans' demands. "Con España, hay que darle candela al jarro hasta que suelte el fondo" (with Spain, you have to keep the pressure on up until the very end) repeated Irene. "Nothing short of independence will work."

Chapter 17

Pilón, June 1865: Worries

Worry is interest paid on trouble before it comes due.
William Ralph Inge

*T*he zafra had run late this year, extending well past the first rains that ushered the onset of the tiempo muerto. Rocha had attributed the delays to various causes, including insufficient available labor, transportation snags, equipment breakdowns. At last, when the final sacks of refined sugar were boarded on the barge that would carry them to Santiago, he visited Cecilia – as he did almost daily – to report on the status of operations at Santa Cruz. "Doña Cecilia," he started, "I have good news and bad news."

Cecilia flinched. She was tired of bad news. "Faustino, please start calling me just Cecilia. What is the news?"

Rocha suppressed a little smile and replied: "My dear lady, I owe you all the respect in the world, but I will abide by your wishes. The good news is that, even though late, the zafra has been excellent, with a total yield seven percent above last year. The increased output will be enough to cover the higher production costs and the drop in the market price of sugar. So, we will end up making the same profit as in 1864."

"What is the bad news?"

"As I warned you when I started work here, some major

equipment repairs will have to be carried out before next year. In particular, the steam engine that powers the crushing mechanism that squeezes juice out of sugarcane stalks is in poor condition and needs to be overhauled. It was made by the firm of Finney & Hoffman, a Brooklyn steam engine manufacturer, but I do not recommend sending it there because of the high cost of shipping; I know of a shop in New Orleans that could do the repairs at a lower cost. With the war in the United States winding down, I can make inquiries as to the feasibility and cost of having our engine overhauled there."

"Faustino, you are the expert. I leave it in your capable hands to do what is needed. How much is it going to cost?"

"Cecilia, I don't know yet, but it will be expensive."

Cecilia sighed. "Well. Go ahead and keep me posted."

"I shall, my lady. But please be aware that there will probably be other repairs to be made in the next few months."

Chapter 18

Pilón, July 1865: A Letter Out of the Blue

Bad news travels at the speed of light;
good news travels like molasses.
Tracy Morgan

New York, New York, April 11, 1865
To: Mrs. Cecilia Serrano
Ingenio Santa Cruz
Pilón, Oriente, Cuba

*D*ear Mrs. Serrano:

I had the honour of making your acquaintance twenty years ago when you and your late husband (may he rest in peace) visited our offices to set up separate trust accounts for your three children, which accounts have been kept in good order since that time. Their balances had been growing substantially up until the onset of the armed conflict that has plagued this nation for the last four years (and, with God's help, appears to have concluded favorably). I expect and look forward to their recovering their pre-war value once the consequences of the war have been overcome.

I am writing in response to your letter of

February 3, 1865, which I just received, inquiring about the possibility of my having met your daughter Graciela in the recent past. I am pleased to inform you that I met Graciela, a charming young lady, last October, when she came to my offices seeking to liquidate the trust fund set in her favor, which she is entitled to do as she is already of legal age. I had the unpleasant duty to advise her that the assets in her trust (and those set for your other children, Carmela and Alberto) are in the form of stock in companies that invested in Southern cotton plantations and are, at the present time, essentially worthless but bound to recover at some point in the future.

Graciela was distressed at the news, but at a subsequent meeting I was able to disburse to her $29.44 from uninvested cash dividends remaining in the trust. Although unhappy with the overall circumstances, I believe she was pleased to receive that sum in cash.

Regarding your inquiry about her current whereabouts, I am sorry to have to let you know that she did not provide me with that information. I expect she will return to our offices at some time in the near future and I will apprise her of your desire that she contact you. She was in good health and fine spirits (except for the adverse financial news) when I last saw her.

I look forward to making your acquaintance again. In the meantime, please feel free to let me know if I can be of any further assistance.

Very truly yours,
Theophilus Davis, RIA

Chapter 19

Pilón, July 1865: Reunion

Family is not an important thing. It's everything.
Michael J. Fox

Cecilia and Carmela sat across from each other in the manor house's oversized dining room, trying to make sense of Mr. Davis' letter and its implications. On the one hand, it was reassuring to know that Graciela was safe—or at least had been safe nine months earlier, when she met with the banker. On the other hand, she was clearly without money and, as far as they knew, had nobody to whom she could turn in that distant land. How was she managing? Was she hungry? Was she safe? Was she … alive?

"Stupid girl!" repeated Carmela.

"I could kick her!" started Cecilia, and then whimpered: "What are we going to do?"

"We?" shot back Carmela. "There is nothing that we, sitting here, can do. Whatever happens to her, she brought it all on herself. She has always been pigheaded, and lesbiana to boot. Let her fend for herself!"

"You never got along with your sister" reproached Cecilia. "But whatever her faults, she is family, and we need to find a way to rescue her!"

"Well, we could try hiring a detective in New York to look

for her."

"But we don't know how to do that" lamented Cecilia, and then her face brightened. "Maybe Faustino can help us!"

"Mother, I am not sure we should trust Rocha with a delicate family matter such as this. We hardly know him."

"With your father and now your uncle gone and Albertico still a child, there are no men to whom we can turn, and Rocha is good and reliable."

Carmela was about to reply when there was a commotion outside.

"There is a carriage at the door," said Carmela.

"Who could it be?"

A few moments later, Yaya came in, panting. Her dark face seemed flushed with excitement. "Doña Cecilia, acaba de llegar …"

"Rodolfo," completed a dust-covered Rodolfo Durán.

***

"You have some nerve to come here uninvited, after all you and your brother have done," scolded Cecilia, instantly incensed.

"Señora, please do not blame me for the deeds of my wayward brother, which I condemn as much as you do" replied Rodolfo. "As for my actions, all I am guilty of is loving your daughter!"

"Please, let's not get into this!" cut in Carmela. "Rodolfo, we are in the middle of a family discussion that does not concern you, so I would appreciate it if you would go back to Yara and come back when we are ready to receive you."

"I rode all night because I must see you and my boys, who you took away from me a year and a half ago. I am not leaving until I talk to them and to you" replied Rodolfo, raising his voice.

"Fifo and Lazarito are fine, resting in their room. I am not about to wake them up for you."

"Carmela, please! They are my children as much as they are yours!"

Carmela noticed the pleading tone in her husband's voice, and was somewhat mollified. "Fine, go back to the drawing room and wait for me to get you there. Mother and I are discussing a serious problem we are having with Graciela."

"Your sister? What's wrong with her?"

Carmela bit her lip at her indiscretion. "Nothing that concerns you."

"Look, anything that happens in this family concerns me."

"Well, fine. Graciela is gone to the United States and we have lost track of her."

"When did she leave?"

"She left for New York in September and we have not heard from her since that time."

Rodolfo gasped. "And you have had no news at all?"

"Yesterday we got a letter from our banker in New York saying that he met her in October but does not know where she is now. He also said she has no money."

"That's terrible," replied Rodolfo. "What are you going to do about it?"

"That's what we were talking about. Mother is thinking of asking our new administrator to help us hire detectives in New York to try to track her down."

"You shouldn't trust a family matter to a stranger you barely know."

"That is what I was thinking, but neither my mother nor I can take care of the situation, and your brother did away with Uncle Leonard, so we are in a bind."

Rodolfo's next words took everyone, including him, by surprise: "I'll go to America to track Graciela for you!"

Cecilia shot back angrily: "Over my dead body!"

Carmela's response was more measured. "That's crazy. You are barely in your twenties, know no English, have never traveled anywhere farther than these mountains, and get terribly seasick, as you did when we took that ride out of Manzanillo. How could you possibly be of any help? And, if you managed to get to that distant big city, you would get lost yourself!"

"All that's true, but I am strong and have my wits and am willing to face any dangers for you and your family."

"And what would you do about your farm? You and I know that *Los Suspiros* does not run itself. I even wonder how you managed to get here today."

"I asked Eusebio to take care of the place for a couple of days. It will be fine just for that while. If I have to be away for longer, I'll ask Doña Isabel to take back my interest in the farm and find someone else to run it for her. Poor woman!"

"And you would do all that for me?"

"That and more, Carmela. You know I love you!!"

"How about those loose women you mess around with?"

"There are no other women!! How many times do I have to tell you? You are all I care for in life!" He made a choking sound.

"Look, sit in the drawing room, and relax for a while. Mother and I have to finish our conversation, and then I will have Mercedes wake up the children and bring them down for you to meet them."

Chapter 20

Pilón, July 1865: Another Arrival

> *To us, family means putting your arms*
> *around each other and being there.*
> Barbara Bush

Rodolfo's meeting with his children proved a moving experience for all. Fifo, now four, was tall for his age and rather thin, and his dark completion and kinky hair betrayed his ancestry. He was old enough to remember his father and clung to Rodolfo's knees desperately as if needing to make sure Rodolfo was not about to leave again. Lazarito was barely two but darted quickly between one and then another of his parents, as if indicating his desire for their being together. Both children were clearly enjoying the occasion and voiced loud protests when Mercedes, their nurse, picked them up and returned them upstairs.

After the children left Rodolfo's eyes were still wet, and Carmela felt an unexpected lump of emotion in her throat. "Why don't you stay in the guest room so you can visit with the children again tomorrow before you go back to Yara?"

Rodolfo squeezed his wife's shoulder in wordless thanks and, as he was being led away by Yaya, the slave muttered: "If you give me your clothes, I'll wash and iron them overnight. In the meantime, I will bring some old clothes of Master Leonardo for you to wear around the house and get you a bite to eat."

The following morning, after another emotional encounter with the children, Rodolfo was finishing a quick breakfast and making ready to depart when there was another arrival at the manor house: Eusebio, the slave Rodolfo had left in charge of the farm, galloped in atop an unfamiliar horse, both rider and mount drenched in sweat after many hours of travel.

Rodolfo ran to the front door to meet him. "Eusebio! What are you doing here? Is there a problem at the farm?"

Eusebio was almost too exhausted to speak but was able to utter two astonishing sentences: "Your brother Rino and his men have taken over *Los Suspiros*. He sent me to tell you that you can spend as much time in Pilón as you want, he'll manage your farm while you are away."

Chapter 21

Pilón, July 1865: Sending Money into the Void

We all need money, but there are degrees of desperation.
Anthony Burgess

"**I need to** get back to Yara," insisted Rodolfo. "I betrayed Doña Isabel's confidence by letting her farm lie in the hands of outlaws. Who knows what damage my crazy brother is causing. Plus, sooner or later, the authorities are going to show up there and who knows what will happen."

Carmela was loath to admit it, but the presence of Rodolfo in her house was great for the children and having him around was somehow reassuring. So she kept suggesting that he stay a couple of more days, and Rodolfo was willing to ignore the cry of his conscience in favor of a few hours of domesticity.

Then came another letter, this one from the vicar of a catholic church in Guantánamo. Its author, a Dominican priest, indicated in a brief cover note that he had received the enclosed correspondence from Friar Bernard O'Donnell, the vicar of the St. Joseph church in New York City, with instructions that the enclosure be forwarded to the Serrano family in Pilón. The enclosure was a letter from Graciela to Cecilia:

Dear Mother:

Every night I fall asleep blaming myself for being so stupid and conceited in thinking I could just say goodbye to my family and to the place I was born and make a new life on my own. I am paying for my arrogance. I am stranded in New York, penniless and depending on the charity of others.

For the moment, I have found a temporary job as a governess and live at the home of my employers. I long to return home, but lack the means, since my trust fund has turned out to be worthless.

I have written you several times but received no response. I imagine the war has caused my letters (and your replies, if any) to be lost. I am hoping the resources of the Catholic Church will result in delivery to you of this letter. If you get it, I beg you to remit the sum of two hundred dollars to Theophilus Davis, the broker who holds the trusts that Father set for us, with instructions that the sum, minus fees, be made available to me on demand. I know it is an exorbitant amount of money, but I promise I will pay the money back to you upon return, no matter how long it takes. In the meantime, hoping that you are all in good health, am looking forward to seeing you soon,

Your prodigal but loving daughter,
Graciela.

New York, April 15, 1865

Cecilia read the letter twice, trying to suppress her tears of joy and relief. Graciela was safe! But there was no time to waste!

Two hundred U.S. dollars was a very large sum, but she expected the family's account with Banco del Comercio would have enough funds for such a transfer, and the bank routinely sent and received funds from the United States. How could she order them right away to make this transfer? Mail service between Pilón and La Habana was carried by ship via Santiago and was slow, and a letter could take three weeks to reach its destination; the service was also unreliable, for it depended on weather conditions and sea currents.

"Why don't you send someone from the mill to La Habana by boat to hand carry the letter, or hire an agent to do it for you?" suggested Carmela.

Rodolfo, who was listening to the conversation, piped in: "I can take it myself. I was willing to go to the United States even by sea, but I can get to La Habana on horseback and should have no problem getting there."

"Would you be willing to do it for us?" questioned Cecilia.

"As I said before, I would do anything for my family" reassured Rodolfo.

"It is very far" replied Cecilia. "It would take you a good two weeks of hard riding."

"I can do that. I'm a good rider."

"Well," considered Cecilia. "My late husband Lázaro, like his father before him, loved traveling and left behind some good maps of Cuba showing the towns all over the island and the roads connecting them. I still keep a couple of them that you could use, although of course you would have to ask for directions frequently. How would you go, on horseback or by carriage?"

Rodolfo was quick to respond: "I have traveled both ways; traveling on horseback is generally faster than traveling by carriage, because a horse can reach higher speeds when ridden directly, while a carriage is typically slower, only reaching speeds comparable to a horse's slow trot."

"I will get you a fine horse for the first part of the trip, and then you can rest it or trade it along the way" offered Cecilia.

"All I need from you is the address where your bank is located and more or less how to get to it once I'm in La Habana" stated Rodolfo confidently, noting to himself how the discussion had drifted from whether he should go to how.

"I can get you that, plus provisions and money for the trip" replied Cecilia.

"I can leave first light tomorrow, if you can get the preparations made."

"I shall really be grateful for this" noted Cecilia.

"I'm happy to do it," replied Rodolfo, "for you … and for Carmela and the family."

Chapter 22

New York, August 1865: A New Acquaintance

I believe in the miracle of chance encounters.
Paulo Coelho

Graciela's duties as governess included taking her charges after breakfast on a walk in Gramercy Park, near the Farnsworth's brownstone. It was a short distance, but it served to further awaken the girls and get them ready for the lessons of the day ahead. The park was privately owned and Graciela had to use a key given to her by Edith Farnsworth to gain access to it.

That day, their routine was finished and Graciela had just locked up and stepped onto the sidewalk outside the park when a voice sounded behind her: "My, your hair is so beautiful!"

Graciela turned around and her eyes met those of a woman in her thirties, with unruly locks, worn upswept, that were starting to show gray. She was dressed in a tailored white shirt and dark blue toe-length skirt, giving off an air of casual elegance, a deliberate departure from the rules of fashion. Surprised, Graciela stammered: "Th...thank you, you are.. too... k... kind." Graciela was not used to being complimented on her appearance for, like her siblings, she had amber skin, slightly slanted eyes, and unremarkable facial features. On the other hand, her kinky hair was raven black, lustrous, and dropped down her shoulders in a short cascade.

The woman insisted "Au contraire, darling. You have an exotic beauty rarely seen in these parts! Are you from Spain?"

Graciela suppressed the frown that was forming around the corners of her mouth and replied brightly: "Close, but not quite. I am from Cuba."

"Cuba! Wonderful! There has been a lot written about Cuba recently in the Times! Welcome to New York! I'm Evelyn; what's your name?"

As she responded: "My name is Graciela Serrano," Graciela felt a shudder course down her spine and a long-suppressed emotion fill her spirit. The image of Ernestina formed behind her eyes; something about this woman reminded her of the love she had left behind. She smiled and asked: "Do you live around here?"

"I have a studio some distance north. I jog on the street to get some exercise."

Graciela had no idea what "jogging" meant but the word "studio" attracted her attention. "What kind of studio?"

Evelyn shrugged her shoulders. "I'm just an ordinary painter. Not of big canvases, but small pieces."

"How interesting" replied Graciela. "I've never seen a painter at work before."

"Oh, you have to come to my studio sometime. I'll give you a tour."

"I'd love that" replied Graciela.

"Do you live around here?" asked Evelyn.

"I live in a brownstone a couple of blocks away. I look after these girls." She pointed to the Farnsworth children, who were fidgeting, waiting for the grownups to finish their talk. "I take them for a walk in the park" she pointed to the Gramercy Park behind her.

"Oh, I have never been inside the park, since it is not open to the public."

"I get in with a key from the lady I work for" replied Graciela. "Do you want to see it?" And then: "I'll trade a tour of the park for one of your atelier."

"Deal!" replied Evelyn enthusiastically. "When do you want to do it?"

"Later today? I get a break at four."

"Great! Meet you here at four."

Chapter 23

Pilón, September 1865: Disappointment

Do not call it sin in me that I am forsworn for thee.
Shakespeare, Love Labour's Lost (Act 4, Scene 3)

Rodolfo **returned to** Pilón after a trip that consumed over a month of his life. He was exhausted, was noticeably thinner, and felt in his bones the remembered pain of hour after hour on the saddle, negotiating steep, muddy, or almost non-existent roads. He had seen a lot of misery among the poor country folk he had met, but who nonetheless had proved uniformly welcoming and generous to a lone traveler. He had once barely escaped capture by bandits by waving and shooting into the air the Colt Dragoon revolver he had purchased in Manzanillo at the onset of his trip. On his return, he remained silent about this incident and the rest of the trip, except to complain that La Habana was a dirty, noisy and fulsome city full of negroes, mulattos and immigrants from all over the world and vowed never to go back to it.

He had, however, delivered a letter of instruction requesting the transfer of two hundred dollars, net of fees and expenses, to the Continental Trust Company of New York City, to be held in escrow for disbursement, all or in part, on demand to Miss Graciela Serrano or anyone else presenting written authorization from one of the following persons: Cecilia Marín, viuda de

Serrano; Carmela Serrano; or Alberto Serrano. The money was already safely on its way to New York, awaiting a request for it from Graciela. All that could possibly be done for her had been accomplished.

He reported the success of his enterprise to Cecilia and Carmela the moment he dismounted from his exhausted steed. When he was done, Cecilia let out a sigh of relief:

"Thank you very much, Rodolfo, for what must have been a burdensome assignment. I must apologize. You are like Abel, and I confused you with the Cain you have for a brother. I am in your debt forever."

"No need to thank me, Mother. I did it for the family, so it was a pleasure as well as an obligation."

"Speaking of family," replied Cecilia, "did you meet Alberto in La Habana?"

"Yes, mother. Seeing him after all these years was the only thing pleasant that happened to me in La Habana."

"How is he doing? Anything new with him? He does not say much in his letters."

Rodolfo thought about the beautiful redhead with whom his friend was living, but he had been sworn to secrecy. "Not much. Law studies are going well and he is getting involved in politics, hanging out with the reformists to see if they can extract concessions from the government in Madrid."

"I wish he would stay out of trouble" replied Cecilia. "We have enough things to worry about."

"Will you rest for a few days before returning to Yara?" cut in Carmela.

"Will you and the children return with me, please?" pleaded Rodolfo again.

Carmela vacillated for a moment and then shook her head in denial.

"No. I can't."

"Why not?"

"Because … I don't love you. Binding my life to yours was a mistake that must be remedied."

Rodolfo's head bowed in defeat and he staggered as if he was about to lose his footing. "I am not going back to the farm. Without you, nothing remains there for me."

There was a brief silence, which Cecilia broke by speaking acidly to her daughter:

"Carmela! How can you be so harsh with this boy, who clearly loves you?"

"Mother, I am being kind. Rodolfo's love is like a sick chicken that needs to be put out of its misery."

It was Rodolfo's time to protest. "So be it. I don't know what I'm going to do, but I won't be separated again from my children. They miss me and need a father. I won't return to Yara."

Cecilia intervened once more. "The pink house to the left of the entrance to the mill is empty. Leonardo used it as a place for business visitors to stay. Rodolfo can stay there as long as he wants as my guest. And he is welcome to come here as often as he wants to see his children. It is the least we can do."

Carmela started to raise an objection but thought better of it. "Fine" she declared.

"Moreover," went on Cecilia, "let me talk to Faustino. There must be a job at the mill for Rodolfo. It would be good to have someone from the family keeping an eye on operations." And it would be good to have a man around the house again, she told herself.

Chapter 24

New York, October 1865: A Move

Every new beginning comes from some other beginning's end.
Seneca

*T*he romance between Graciela and Evelyn exploded after a series of furtive encounters in the privacy of Gramercy Park, where they met in mid-afternoons when the regular park visitors were still at work. It had taken only one such meeting to establish that they had the same sexual predilections and were attracted to each other, and from then on, they proceeded to explore each other with gusto.

In the course of developing an intimate friendship, Graciela felt the need to confide in Evelyn on her increasingly difficult employment situation. Graciela's arrangement as live-in governess felt less tolerable with each passing day. Edith Farnsworth had quickly shown her true colors, becoming demanding, domineering and abusive towards her captive employee; in an opposing trend, her husband had started to make surreptitious moves to gain Graciela's favors – a knowing smile here, a brush of her cheek, an indiscreet touching or rubbing of the girl's backside; it was obvious that Edward Farnsworth was just waiting for the right opportunity to make a move on Graciela. She tried to ignore or politely reject his advances, but the cat and mouse game was taxing on Graciela's nerves and making her increasingly worried.

"I'm afraid to offend my employers" explained Graciela after describing her situation. "They are powerful people and if they get cross with me, they could throw me on the streets or even get me arrested on some trumped-up charge."

Evelyn offered: "Just move in with me and become my assistant. I can't pay you much, but from what you tell me those highfaluting folks are not too generous, either."

"I would not want to impose on your kindness" started Graciela, and interrupted herself. "It's terrible to be without money and not get a word from my family. I want to go back to Cuba!"

"I can't help you get back to Cuba, but how about a shorter move, uptown? I promise you will enjoy it better than your current situation."

A few days later, matters came to a head. Mrs. Farnsworth announced that she was taking her daughters on a trip to Philadelphia to spend a few days with her family. "I can take care of the girls, so you don't have to come. Stay in town and treat this as a short vacation."

Graciela panicked. The following afternoon, she told Evelyn of her fears. "I am sure that Mr. Farnsworth will attack me while his wife is away. She is too cheap to pay for my travel, and too stupid not to think of the risk to which she is exposing me."

"I have a different theory" replied Evelyn. "Their sex life has probably dried out and she is thinking of tossing him a bone to keep him contented."

Graciela drew a deep intake of breath. "Do you think they could be so base?"

"Sure. You are a nobody. A homeless girl from a Spanish backwater, totally beneath their class. His seducing you wouldn't even be considered cheating!"

"What can I do?"

"As I offered before, come to live with me. I can have a carriage at your door in a couple of hours. You have nothing to lose, so come with me."

Graciela remembered well how harshly she had criticized Carmela for her elopement with Rodolfo Durán and felt guilty about taking a similarly impetuous course of action. But, of course, she herself had left Cuba on impulse, so it was not much more she could do that would be worse.

"Alright, but send the carriage tonight, at nine or so, after dinner. I don't want to have a farewell scene with those people. I'd rather sneak out."

***

Graciela celebrated the anniversary of her arrival in the United States in Evelyn's apartment, midway up an Eighth Avenue light-colored brick building full of artist studios—painters like Evelyn, as well as sculptors, musicians, and dancers. She had soon adapted to a bohemian lifestyle that went well with her predilections, and in addition to assisting her friend with the mechanical parts of a painter's work, she was learning basic ceramics techniques. She had not received any news from her family and had stopped going to Theophilus Davis' offices once her cash account was emptied.

So far, her life as Evelyn's lover and assistant had gone well, and the two of them took in as much of New York's cultural and artistic life as time and budget allowed. Thus, it came as a shock when, at the end of the small party to celebrate Graciela's coming into the country, Evelyn proposed: "What would you think about moving upstate to one of the new art colonies that are springing up all over this part of the United States? I have heard of a farm near Woodstock where artists, writers, musicians, and others are moving to live more cheaply in a beautiful rural setting, away from the city's noise and commotion."

Graciela instantly recalled the family's move to Pilón a decade earlier and her years of exile in the "dark provinces," and was revolted by the idea of repeating that experience. She almost

153

screamed: "No way! No more life in the boondocks for me! I love New York and want to stay here!"

Evelyn realized she had hit a raw nerve and did not insist. Graciela was easy to convince, given enough time and a gentle touch.

Chapter 25

Pilón, November 30, 1865: More Expenditures

A shippe and a woman are ever repairing.
George Herbert

As the faithful were getting ready for the Advent season, Cecilia tried to get in a holiday mood by planning the festivities for the upcoming holidays. She was in the midst of drawing an invitee list for the Christmas Eve dinner when Yaya ushered in a flustered looking Faustino Rocha, who omitted his usual pleasantries and got right to the point: "Cecilia, we have a problem. The zafra is just starting and we have a major equipment failure!"

"Another one?" replied Cecilia, alarmed. She was still reeling from the cost of repairing the steam engine and was not sure the business could afford another big equipment expenditure.

"It won't be as bad as having to overhaul the steam engine, but potentially costly because of the timing."

"What's the matter with the timing?"

"As you know, the casa de calderas is where the cane juice coming from the grinding mill is clarified and concentrated by forcing it by means of pumps into large kettles known as defecadoras, that is, clarifiers. We have two pumps for each clarifier, to allow for maintenance or repairs to one of them without stopping the entire juice clarification process. One of these pumps just failed and needs to be replaced right away for if we lose the other, the mill operation will slow down considerably. Normally the pump replacement can be done at relatively low cost during the tiempo muerto, but doing so as an urgent matter during the zafra puts us at the mercy of the suppliers, who can inflate prices to take advantage of our predicament."

"Well, but can you get the pump replaced for us in short order?"

"I can send an urgent order to the same New Orleans outfit that overhauled the steam engine and get a new one by the end of the year. That way we would be at risk only during the next month."

"Well, I guess we'll have to do it."

"I agree, but I must warn you, it will be expensive."

"I hear you. Go ahead and put the order in."

"Thank you, Cecilia. I'll talk to you later."

As she watched Rocha run away, Cecilia went back to her invitee list. "We are going broke. We must start skimping." She restarted the list, paring it down to only eight couples. "Better they think me cheap than watch us go to the poorhouse."

Chapter 26

La Habana, December 1865: An Invitation

One's destination is never a place, but a new way of seeing things.
Henry Miller

As was his usual way, Carlos barged into Alberto's room without knocking, almost catching the couple in the act of making love. Noting Alberto's surprise and Irene's annoyance, Carlos apologized profusely but, almost in the same breath, delivered the news that had him so excited.

"Guys, I'm going to Spain!"

"Taking another trip?" wondered Alberto. "You just came back from visiting your family in Bayamo."

"Exactly" beamed Carlos. "Remember how last month the Queen appointed Antonio Cánovas del Castillo as Foreign Minister, and Cánovas announced the formation of a council, a Junta de Información, to look into the changes that should be made to Spain's administration of Cuba?"

"Yes, another farce," replied Irene acidly.

"Well, maybe," went on Carlos. "Anyhow, the Junta is to be comprised of Spanish government officials and representatives from Cuba's municipalities, sixteen of them altogether. José

Antonio Saco was elected to represent Santiago de Cuba in the Junta, and my uncle Bartolomé offered to pay for my going to Spain with Saco as his secretary so I can keep track of what goes on for him, and Saco accepted. So, I am bound for Madrid early next year."

"Congratulations," replied Alberto, warmly. "I hope you have a good time, but make sure to take warm clothes. I hear that Madrid can get very cold in the winter."

"Well, you are going to have to do the same," replied Carlos with a slick smile.

"What?"

"When Uncle Bartolomé offered to send me to Spain, I said I would be too lonely there and insisted that you accompany me. My uncle demurred at first because he is not that wealthy, but he likes you and finally acceded. So, you are coming with me! We'll have a ball!"

Alberto turned pale. "Me, go to Madrid? For how long?"

"I don't know, it could be several months. Those councils often spend a long time studying things."

"How about my studies?"

"I'm sure the Law School will still be there when you get back."

"But wait, I'm not going to leave Irene alone for all that time!"

Irene interjected a caustic remark: "Sure, I'll start letting boys up my window the moment you take off!"

Alberto blushed. "I didn't mean that. I know you'be faithful. But it wouldn't be fair to abandon you for such a long time!"

"I'm the one who should worry. Knowing you, the first gypsy tart to make eyes at you will get you into her bed."

Alberto started a denial, but she cut him off: "And I don't care. Be a puto if you want, but come back alive and don't catch anything there and give it to me."

"Do you mean you don't mind if I spend some time abroad?"

"I do mind, but I am thinking of what is good for you. You are still a babe and need to learn a bit about the world. As long as you are healthy, I am worried only about one thing about your going to that Junta."

"What?"

"You and the other Cuban suckers are going to be disappointed. Spain will never do anything for Cuba except bleed us dry."

Chapter 27

Pilón, December 31, 1865: New Year Blues

An optimist stays up until midnight to see the new year in.
A pessimist stays up to make sure the old year leaves.
Bill Vaughan

*C*ecilia sat alone on the blue drawing room divan, melancholically swallowing the grapes of good fortune whole, without tasting them. It had been a difficult year and her affairs – business and personal – were in increasing disarray. One of her children had been lost without a trace, another was bound for a potentially long stay an ocean away. The third one was clinging to her rancor against her estranged husband and no longer made a pretense of helping out with family matters.

The only bright spots in her life were her grandchildren, sweet and alert and growing like weeds. Their father came often to see them and tonight he had taken them out to see the end of year festivities, but otherwise his visits were marred by the wall of ice Carmela had erected to keep Rodolfo at bay.

Business was also a source of heartache. Rocha was keeping the zafra going, but between equipment repairs, a drop in the price of sugar, the cost of replacing the dwindling slave labor force, and increased taxation by the rapacious Spanish government, the sugar mill's balance sheet was showing red, and she felt that the enterprise her brother-in-law Leonardo had built was on the verge of collapsing.

She remembered the night, six years before, when she and Alberto had sat until midnight to greet the new decade with hope in their hearts. The sixties were halfway gone leaving very little to show for the troubles they had brought. But, as she always did, Cecilia resolved to soldier on and put a brave face on the family's misfortunes. She felt inadequate to meet her burdens, but there was nobody else. Perhaps things would turn around.

She finished the last grape, said a silent prayer to Saint Jude, the patron saint of desperate causes, and went upstairs to spend another night alone in her chambers.

Part 3

1868

A Long War Ahead

Chapter 1

Pilón, February 11, 1866: Limping Along

The struggle itself toward the heights is enough to fill a man's heart. One must imagine Sisyphus happy.

Albert Camus

Cecilia Serrano had come to dread the visits from Faustino Rocha. It was not that the sugar mill's administrator was rude or demanding; to the contrary, Faustino was polite to the point of unctuousness and always treated the owner of *Santa Cruz* with greatest deference. All the same, the appearance of the neat, balding man at the door of the manor house was a harbinger of trouble, for it meant that there was some difficulty at the mill that could only be cured through the expenditure of a good bit of money.

Therefore, one could not blame the widowed head of the family for greeting the underling with little warmth. "Hello, Faustino. Anything wrong at the mill?"

Rocha grinned. "No, my dear lady." Cecilia's narrowed brow

gave away her impatience, and the man continued quickly. "The zafra is going well, but I must report a concern I may have raised before about plant security."

"What do you mean?"

"There have been reports of strangers walking around the mill and its immediate areas. I don't need to remind you of the potential risks to property and the safety of personnel, let alone your own, that such a situation poses."

Cecilia's shoulder bore the scar left by the shot that had been fired at her six years earlier, and the memory of the other shot that eventually killed her brother-in-law was still vivid in her mind. "I know" she replied briskly. "What should we do about it?"

"I know this retired captain in Holguín that runs a firm that hires out bodyguards to wealthy individuals and businesses. I can contact him to see if he can provide some guards under contract."

"How many would we need?"

"At least three, but I would have to discuss it with him."

"Why can't we hire guards ourselves?"

"I wouldn't know how to go about picking security personnel."

"Alright. Go ahead and talk to your contact. How much is it going to cost us?"

"I don't know yet. I will go to Holguín over the weekend and let you know."

"I hope it is not too much. Our finances are in poor shape, you know."

"I know, and am very sorry. I do my best to economize, but running a sugar mill is expensive these days."

Rocha took his leave and Cecilia was left ruing once again Leonardo's interdiction of the sale of the mill years before, when the going was good. Had they gotten rid of this accursed business, she and her children (perhaps even Graciela) would be together, in peace and prosperity, enjoying life again in La Habana. The years of her captivity weighed more each day she remained in this remote corner of the island.

Chapter 2

New York, February 15, 1866: Cuban Contacts

We are linked by blood, and blood is memory without language.
Joyce Carol Oates

One good thing about living in an apartment building full of artists was the opportunity to meet all sorts of fascinating men and women, each with his or her own particular interests and unique life experiences. Graciela was not gregarious by nature, but she could not help chatting with these people and listening to the unique stories they had to tell.

It was at one of these informal parties in the loft of a painter friend of her bedmate Evelyn that Graciela met an unprepossessing middle-aged man who was making the rounds, stopping at each table to exchange a few words with one or another of the guests. It was clear that he knew everyone and everybody knew him. When he arrived at the table where Graciela sat alone (Evelyn was working late that evening) the man removed his bowler hat and bowed to her: "How can it possibly be that such a beautiful lady would be allowed to sit alone? Would you honor me by permitting that I sit next to you?"

Graciela, taken by surprise, just nodded in acquiescence. As he pulled up a chair and sat next to her, the man introduced himself grandly: "I am Felix Grillo, but everyone in this entire town calls me "Cricket" because of my last name. To whom do I have the honor of speaking?"

"My name is Graciela Serrano."

"Oh, a Latin beauty. I am Latin also, from Guatemala. How about you?"

"I'm from Cuba."

Felix's eyes widened in surprise, followed by a wide grin.

"Cubana! Only the other evening I spent a few hours in the company of a dozen of your compatriots. Such delightful people!"

"What do you mean?"

"Well, darling, you should know that I am a writer of works of fiction, specializing in historical novels. It is a difficult trade these days because most well-known places in the world – England, France, Italy, even Russia – have already been milked for their histories by other writers. For that reason, I am always in search of exotic places that may yield interesting new tales. So, when I learned that the people at the Ateneo Democrático Cubano de Nueva York were presenting another of their lectures on Cuban history I rushed to attend. You know, the Ateneo has been doing this for a number of years."

"Did you learn any good stories about Cuba?"

The expression in the man's face darkened a little. "No, Cuba does not seem to have had any great historical events worth writing about. All they seem to be talking about these days is slavery and the efforts needed to end it. But I met several interesting people, in particular this man Juan Manuel Macías, who announced to the attendees that he had founded a group named the "Sociedad Republicana de Cuba y Puerto Rico" intended to work towards gaining independence for both islands. Have you heard about Macías?"

"I am sorry. I don't follow Cuban politics."

"You would like Macías. A very engaging man." Felix dug into the inner pocket of his frock coat and extracted a large black leather case bulging with calling cards of all colors and sizes.

Rummaging through its contents, he triumphantly extracted one and presented it to Graciela: "Here, in case you want to meet one of your compatriots."

Graciela felt it would not be polite to turn down Grillo's offer, so she picked up the card and buried it in her rose beaded purse. As she did, she felt a momentary pang of nostalgia remembering her quince celebration in La Habana a decade earlier; then, the reminiscence passed.

Chapter 3

Pilón, April, 1866: Recriminations

One doesn't wish to see those to whom one owes so much.
Pierre Corneille

As was now frequent between them, mother and daughter were arguing over Carmela's high-handed treatment of her estranged husband. "It took me a while to appreciate Rodolfo's goodness, but I will forever be thankful for all he has done for this family" repeated Cecilia. "Not only did he give up a month of his life just to make sure money was available to your sister, but he gave up his business and home in Yara to be here, near you and his children. What other proof of his love and devotion could you possibly want?"

"It is not that I don't appreciate what he has done and continues to do. For one thing, his children adore him and having him around has had a great positive change in their lives. But it is just that I never loved him and would like nothing more than for him to go away and leave me alone. As long as he is hovering around our lives, I can't feel free to be myself. That's the problem, and it is never going to change."

"But," Cecilia said, "he has agreed to work for us in the sugar mill and has taken over, at my request, responsibility for the maintenance of equipment, carpentry and other support functions, and oversight of those repairs of machinery that can be performed onsite. He also helps keep an eye on what Rocha does, which is a godsend since neither I nor you can second-guess the man. Even if you didn't appreciate Rodolfo as a lover, you should be eternally grateful for all he is doing for us."

"Again, if he were a complete stranger I would be grateful. But, still, he looks at me with this hangdog expression, like a horse that keeps getting beaten and is still faithful to its master. I can't stand not being able to reciprocate, nor put him out of his misery somehow."

"Let me tell you something" replied Cecilia. "No marriage is perfect, no man is without flaws. Take your father, for instance. Lázaro was a decent man, faithful, a good provider. Yet he was not affectionate to me and, like his father before him, got more pleasure from roaming the world than in spending time with his family. I tolerated all his coldness and his other faults because, on the whole, he was a good spouse and gave me three children to love. Rodolfo is every bit as good, if no better, than your father was."

"Well, he cheated on me ..." argued Carmela.

"So you say" countered Cecilia. "This has not been proved. Anyhow, can you blame him for minor infidelities given how cold you have been with him almost from the start?"

"Mother, we are never going to agree on this. I will tolerate having him around, but neither he nor you can expect more."

Chapter 4

La Habana, September, 1866: Time to Go

Delay always breeds danger.
Miguel de Cervantes

*T*he contingent of Cuban representatives in the Junta de Información that was to consider changes to Spain's colonial regime was selected on March 25, 1866; twelve of the sixteen representatives of Cuba's municipalities were members of the Reform party, of which Alberto Serrano and his friend Carlos Masó were members. However, in the first half of 1866 Spain experienced serious political unrest, including an uprising led by General Juan Prim and a revolt at the San Gil barracks in Madrid. These events caused a delay in the initiation of the Junta's activities.

As a result of the unrest, there was a change in government and the Unión Liberal Party that had sponsored the creation of the Junta was ousted from power in July 1866 and replaced by a "moderado" party that was unsympathetic to the calls for change in Cuba's administrative regime. Nonetheless, the new Spanish rulers decided to convene the Junta and ordered it to start its meetings on October 30.

The long delay and the change in government were seen by many as potential death blows to the efforts to bring about positive changes in Cuba. Nonetheless, in accordance with the old Spanish saying that "no hay peor gestión que la que no se hace" (there is no worse undertaking than one that is not carried out), the Cuban delegation decided to go forward with the meetings in Madrid. Alberto and Carlos remained sanguine about the prospects for progress and finally left for Spain in early September.

Alberto's girlfriend Irene went to see them board the steamship that would carry them across the ocean. Her eyes were dry and her mouth pursed into a thin line. She had no hopes that anything good would come out of the meetings in Madrid and, in the best possible case, Alberto would return to her in good health but with hopes dashed. She would be waiting, ready to console him.

Chapter 5

New York, Fall, 1866: Moving to the Country

Courage is going from failure to failure without losing enthusiasm.
Winston Churchill

*G*raciela **resisted for** as long as she could Evelyn's suggestions that they leave the tumult of living in the big city for the peace and quiet of the country. However, when the summer of 1866 ended and the economy continued to recover from the Civil War dislocations, New York City landlords sought to make up for lost business by announcing steep rent increases that affected all rental properties, whether lower class tenements or middle-class or better apartment buildings. Thus, it came as no surprise when the landlord of the Eighth Avenue building where Evelyn had her studio announced an almost doubling of the rent each tenant would have to pay.

Evelyn was outraged. "I barely earn enough to keep us fed and clothed, and you are still not making anything with your pottery. We have to move upstate. That is, I have to move. You can go with me or stay in town, it's up to you to decide."

"Can we wait a couple of months to see if our business picks up? The city is growing, they say there are almost a million people in New York these days. You should be able to sell more of your paintings."

"Bahh" replied Evelyn. "Most of the newcomers are indigents, immigrants who can't afford to buy art." She stopped for a second, realizing she had probably insulted Graciela. Then she went on: "I have contacted a real estate agent to find us a cottage in the Woodstock area. We should know what's available in a few days. Then you will need to decide what you want to do."

Graciela was not offended by Evelyn's derogatory remark, but the conversation set her mind in motion in an unexpected direction. How did she really feel about Evelyn? Their life together was cozy, the sex was good, and the two of them were in most respects compatible. But did she love Evelyn? The answer was probably not. Certainly not as much affection as she had felt for Ernestina Cueto, and she had not hesitated to leave Ernestina behind…

On the other hand, she was still out of money and returning to the Farnsworths, even if it were feasible, would be unacceptable. Perhaps she should not rush into things again. "Alright, let's give Woodstock a try. But I'm not staying there forever if I don't like it."

"Nothing in life is forever" replied Evelyn.

***

With surprising speed, the real estate agent was able to identify a property in Woodstock that had gone on the rental market earlier in the year. It was a two-story bungalow located a short walk from the center of the village. It featured a large wood-burning, cast-iron stove that could heat the whole house and southern facing windows that bathed the living areas in sunlight, providing a nice working space for painting indoors. It had a generously-sized yard and was surrounded by woods and offered pleasant views of the Catskill mountains, ideal for the type of landscape painting on which Evelyn desired to specialize. It was offered on a three-year lease at a monthly rent much lower than that of the loft in Manhattan. Evelyn loved the description of the property and was immediately ready to sign the lease.

Graciela, however, had reservations. The idea of chopping and carrying large quantities of wood to fire the stove was totally alien to her; she feared that the other rustic features of the property, yet to be revealed, would impose burdens to which she was not accustomed. She saw herself becoming a charwoman, spending her days cleaning, cooking, and doing domestic work of the type that Yaya and other slaves had performed in her earlier life. Woodstock might turn out to be an artistic paradise for her lover, but it might become a penal colony for her.

But it was too late. She had made a commitment to give Woodstock a try. Hopefully, they would be settled in this rented bungalow before the worst of the winter weather set in.

Chapter 6

Madrid, December, 1866: Trying to Tell our Story

*We will try to persuade with our words, but if our
words fail, we will try to persuade with our acts.*
Martin Luther King

*D*ear Irene:

It has been a full month since the Junta began its business. The delegates from Cuba have prepared several documents (in whose drafting I had a minor role) presenting our demands and the reasons supporting them in the three main areas of concern to us: the need to modify the oppressive taxation and governance structures that are strangling us, the need to provide Cuban representation in the Cortes, and the need to put an end to slavery in the island.

Sad to say, even though our papers have been submitted in writing, we have not been allowed to participate in the Junta's meetings. To make matters worse, no written minutes of the Junta's proceedings are being generated and there is a prohibition against public disclosure of the Junta's deliberations. For that reason, we have no idea whether our views are being considered or acted upon.

You, of course, were apparently right in predicting that nothing useful would come out of this initiative of the former government. Either the Junta was convened just for show, to give the appearance that our grievances were being considered, or what was intended as a genuine effort of the Union Liberal has been thwarted by the moderados.

I am not despairing yet, but most of the sixteen members of our delegation are pessimistic about the outcome of the Junta's work. We will persist, however, for as long as there is a chance that something useful will result that will improve life on our island.

Madrid is cold and gloomy this season. Efforts have been going on for several years to expand the city and modernize it so it becomes the equal of London or Paris. It is clear, however, that the country is broke and suffering from successive episodes of civil unrest, which is perhaps part of the reason why its government is set on exploiting its few remaining colonies.

Outside the government, however, the madrileños are friendly, open, and fun-loving; not at all like the types that are sent to Cuba from the provinces to make a fortune at our expense.

I miss you more than words can express and can't wait for the day when I will have you in my arms again. Love you forever,

Alberto

Chapter 7

Madrid, April 28, 1867: Coming Home

If not us, who? If not now, when?
John F. Kennedy

*D*ear Irene:

I have good news and bad news.

The good news first. In a couple of days I will get on a boat bound for La Habana. You may see me before this letter reaches you, but I am penning it just in case.

It will have been six months since I saw you last, but it has felt like an eternity. I swear I will never be away from you again for any length of time. Let us have a big celebration when I get home.

Now the bad news. As you predicted, the Junta de Información, which formally ended yesterday, was a complete fiasco. Five months of work and thirty-six meetings for nothing. Ramón Narváez, the current Prime Minister, formally closed the proceeding, vowing that Minister of the Colonies Alejandro de Castro will perform a detailed review of all the submissions and take appropriate measures; whether this happens or not is of no consequence because it seems certain that no action will be taken on any of our demands.

To the contrary, instead of satisfying our pleas for lowering taxes and custom duties, the government announced new, higher taxes on real estate, income, and business profits. And, instead of curbing the dictatorial powers of the Capitanes Generales who can rule by decree, declare martial law, censor the press, prohibit public gatherings, and summarily imprison political opponents, the ruling party is considering bringing back later in the year Francisco Lersundi for a second term as governor – notwithstanding that Lersundi is hated in Cuba for his despotic earlier rule and ultraconservative views.

I have been left agreeing with the reaction of one of the Cuban representatives to the Junta, Calixto Bernai, who has written:"the role of words is over: it is time to achieve our goals by the sword."

We will talk more when I return, but I now perceive my duty to work towards complete independence of Cuba from Spain.

So, you were right all along. Love forever,

Alberto.

Chapter 8

Pilón, May, 1867: A Poor Zafra

*I can't change the direction of the wind,
but I can adjust my sails to always reach my destination.*
Jimmy Dean

Weather during the tiempo muerto had been unusually hot and dry, resulting in a low yield of the sugar cane that was planted in the summer months and then harvested during the zafra. Faustino Rocha had a melancholic report as the mill's operations came to an end: "This year's sugar output will be a quarter less than last year. We will barely meet operating costs."

"What does that mean for next year?" replied Cecilia.

"We may not have enough money to pay for the repairs that will need to be made before the next harvest. You may need to get a loan to cover the expenses."

"But won't that increase the chances that we will again be in the red this time next year?"

"Cecilia, I'll be honest with you. I saw the same thing happen at Las Maracas, my last place of employment. Once a sugar mill starts losing money, it is difficult for it to become solvent again. I will take a look at what needs to be done and will report back to you in a couple of weeks."

Cecilia wiped a tear with a lace handkerchief. "Ay, Faustino! Lázaro or Leonardo would know what to do, but I am just a poor woman and don't know how to navigate in a man's world. I keep trying to sell this business, but nobody is buying because taxes are too high and the Americans are buying less of our sugar and growing their own. I feel trapped!"

"Now, Cecilia, don't lose faith. Maybe things will turn around."

"I have been waiting and hopping for almost ten years now, ever since my brother-in-law took that bullet."

"I'll try to think of something that may be done to help. Give me a few days, please."

"Thank you, Faustino, but I doubt there is much you can do for me."

"You are probably right, but you are worth my efforts. Let's wait and see."

Chapter 9

Woodstock, New York, June, 1867: Three Seasons in the Country

*The art of living in a small town is one
of the most difficult to acquire.*
Doris Lessing

*G*raciela had endured two and a half seasons of hard living in their Woodstock bungalow, fighting the snow, the freezing cold, and the biting winds coming off the northern New York hills. She had axed limbs off the nearby trees and carried them and other fallen branches back to feed the stove that had kept her and Evelyn alive through subzero temperatures. She had cleaned the rough-hewn barnwood paneling, wiped the wide-plank pinewood flooring, cooked simple meals in the miniscule kitchen nook, washed and dried above the stove countless loads of linens and garments, done scores of burdensome and distasteful chores. Evelyn, on the other hand, had done a few chores but spent most of the time creating oil paintings and watercolors of varying degrees of distinction.

The inequality of their situation had not been lost on Graciela. She had followed her lover out of the city in the hope that country living would be a professional and financial step forward for her; neither of those goals had yet been achieved. Although they had inserted themselves into the village's tightly-knit artistic colony, no commissions for Evelyn's paintings or sales of Graciela's earthenware had materialized.

With the good summer weather, however, hope was rekindled in her heart. The first real opportunity to make contacts with the town's leading residents came at the end of May when a Summer Reception and Cotillon was held at the recently opened Mead's Mountain House hotel, located at the foot of the trail to the Overlook Mountain. There, Evelyn and Graciela were able to meet and spend time over beers and hard ciders with the village moneyed elders, as well as fellow artists of various callings.

Graciela had few occasions to attend dancing parties since her adolescent days and enjoyed twirling around with young and not so young local men. Evelyn, on the other hand, spent the evening making herself known to her potential clients and colleagues. As the evening wore on Graciela – who was feeling woozy from too much hard cider – noticed that Evelyn was spending a lot of time chatting with a young woman named Susie who, like Evelyn, was a landscape painter. Graciela did not want to interrupt the conversation between the two women – which had evolved into a lecture by Susie on the pleasures of hiking the local mountains – but, feeling increasingly ill, came up to the corner where they had retreated and announced that she was feeling a little peaked and wished to go home.

"Go ahead, Graciela, go lie down. I will join you in a bit."

Graciela was disappointed to be sent home alone, but was in no condition to argue, so she said her goodbyes to the people she had met and retreated to their bungalow, where she collapsed into their bed. She sunk into an alcoholic stupor and did not even notice Evelyn's return, much later.

Chapter 10

La Habana, October, 1867: Unrest

*The pessimist complains about the wind; the optimist
expects it to change; the realist adjusts the sails.*
William Arthur Ward

Upon his return to La Habana, Alberto Serrano became
aware of the death of the reformist movement that had sought
to secure political and economic concessions from Spain. The
failure of the Junta de Información and the imposition of even
heavier taxes by the government in Madrid quashed any hopes
of fairer treatment from Spain's conservative rulers. El Siglo, the
organ of the reformer movement, had become discredited and
was closing.

On the other hand, the need for independence from Spain
was getting more acceptance among the wealthiest and better
educated criollos. As a result, the two most recent Spanish governors -- Joaquín del Manzano and, upon his death in office, his

temporary successor, Blas Villate, had spent much time tracking down conspiracies and sending reports to the Minister of the Colonies in Madrid of budding insurrectionist efforts.

Alberto soon became connected with the underground circles that were promoting armed insurrection. His girlfriend (now fiancée) Irene and his childhood friend Carlos Masó were part of the conspiracy.

However, the move towards independence was stronger in the eastern half of the island, particularly the Oriente province where Alberto and Carlos had been raised. In July, a "Revolutionary Committee of Bayamo" had been founded under the leadership of Cuba's wealthiest plantation owner, Francisco Vicente Aguilera. The conspiracy was rapidly spreading to Oriente's larger towns, most of all Manzanillo. Carlos commented: "We may need to go back home if we are going to be useful. Here in La Habana, our efforts are going to be doomed by the police, the Spanish voluntarios, and the spies they plant everywhere." Alberto was not quite ready to return to his mother without having completed his education, but Irene joined Carlos in demanding that Alberto stop thinking about himself and begin putting Cuba's needs in the front burner.

"I will do nothing until I at least finish this year at the law school" replied Alberto. "Unless civil war erupts, my civic duty can wait until next year's summer vacation."

Carlos and Irene were disappointed, but went along with Alberto's plan.

Chapter 11

Pilón, October, 1867: A Chance Encounter

Choose your bedfellows by day.
Swedish Proverb

*T*he three guards that Faustino Rocha hired to provide security at the sugar mill were strong and intimidating specimens of manhood. They were, however, vastly different in appearance. The leader, Lester, was a Jamaican mulatto of medium height but seemed shorter than he actually was because he was an almost perfect cube of muscle, with a face that was hidden by a grayish beard. Luc was a huge, coal black, ugly and muscular Haitian who spoke unintelligible Spanish. Language was generally no problem with him, however, for Luc was a man of few words. And then there was Yoyi.

Yoyi (Jorge Luis Alvarado) was born in the Dominican Republic, and was the youngest and only native Spanish speaker of the trio, so he often served as spokesman for the group. Yoyi was one of those miracles that only the tropics can produce, a perfect blend of the White, the Black, and the Indian, with a smattering of Chinese thrown in. He was of medium height, a bit stocky but powerfully built, and had unruly jet-black hair, slightly slanted brown eyes, full sensuous lips, a snub nose and light cinnamon skin. He was starting to grow a goatee but otherwise was clean-cut, and his features suggested a good nature inside the bulk.

The guards included the manor house in their rounds, so one or another of them would be seen circling the mansion a couple of times a day. Cecilia and Carmela got used to their presence and ignored them until one afternoon, when Carmela was out in the garden with her children. Lazarito, who was almost six, ran blindly into one of the guards making the rounds and ended up sprawled on the dirt. The guard, Yoyi, helped the boy up gently and asked: "Are you ok, son?" to which Lazarito replied, confused, "I dunno …" He was on the verge of tears.

Yoyi responded admiringly: "Well, you were running sooo fast! I've never seen a kid run that fast!" Lazarito's face broke into a smile.

Carmela approached the pair and took Lazarito by the hand. "I am sorry … these kids will be the death of me…" she apologized.

"There is no reason to apologize. Your children are very nice."

Carmela started to reply: "Thank you very much …" but Yoyi continued: "Almost as nice as their mother."

There was a momentary pause, during which Carmela and Yoyi looked at each other. Carmela was startled, for she was reminded for one moment of a sunset eight years before, when she had taken a close look at her future husband for the first time. Yoyi was very handsome, as much as Rodolfo had been, and the recognition made her feel somehow guilty.

"I was about to bring the kids in, it's time for their merienda" she explained, unnecessarily. And then: "Would you like to come in for a cup of coffee and a macaroon?"

"Thank you, ma'am, but I'm on duty."

"Oh, come on! It will be only one minute."

Yoyi seemed to engage in a silent debate with himself, but finally answered: "Alright, but just for one minute." And then he added: "Many thanks. You're very kind."

Chapter 12

Woodstock, New York, November, 1867: As the First Snows Fall

*I like these cold, gray winter days. Days like
these let you savor a bad mood.*
Bill Watterson

Summer and fall rushed by without leaving a trace. Evelyn had gotten a commission to paint the portrait of a wealthy Woodstock matron and was gone much of the day, leaving Graciela alone to perform the housework and carry out her pottery tasks: forming the clay into the shape of the desired vessel, allowing the formed clay to dry, and heating the clay on the stove to harden it. She was still inexperienced, and her most successful efforts involved making jewelry and soap dishes and candle holders; for the upcoming holidays, she was experimenting with the fashioning of necklace pendants and Christmas ornaments which she hoped to sell at the upcoming holiday bazaars.

She did not miss Evelyn that much on weekdays, but she had a growing problem about the weekends. Evelyn had taken to going on mountain treks with her friend and fellow painter

Susie, who was an expert hiker. For those trips, which usually ran into Sunday afternoons, Evelyn had adopted Susie's choice of outside garb: shortened skirts paired with trousers, heavy flannel coats, and sturdy boots. So dressed, the two women looked more like lumberjacks than refined ladies of society.

Graciela was not jealous of the closeness that was obviously growing between Evelyn and Susie; she did not love Evelyn and had developed a domestic partnership with her out of necessity. However, she felt she was being eased out of the arrangement that had brought them into the wilds, and dreaded the idea of returning to her days as a domestic employee, a household servant only a notch or two better than a slave. Having Evelyn gone in the company of another woman for most of the weekend played into her destitution fears.

She felt the world starting to collapse around her when, a cold Friday evening in mid-November, Evelyn declared between gulps of Mulligan stew: "I won't be home Sunday night. Susie and I are going on the Overlook Mountain and Echo Lake trail tomorrow and may camp out both nights. I will see you Monday morning when I come home to clean up and get dressed for work."

The first snow of the season had just fallen and Graciela suspected that, instead of camping out on the cold frozen ground, the women would spend much of the weekend in Susie's in-town lodgings. She protested, perhaps a bit louder than she intended: "And what am I to do with myself in the meantime?"

Evelyn gave her young mate a surprised stare and replied carelessly: "I don't know. Go into town. Read one of my books. Why don't you write a poem, as you say you used to do?"

"My English is not good enough to write fancy poems."

"Well, write it in Spanish. Practice your native language so you don't lose it."

Graciela clenched her teeth and said nothing.

Later on, as she lay awake next to a snoring Evelyn, Graciela tried to recall the last time she had talked to anyone in Spanish. After a while, she concluded that her last Spanish conversation had been with that funny guy from Guatemala, Felix Grillo, who called himself "the Cricket." Felix had mentioned the name of some Cuban who headed an organization in New York City and given her the fellow's card. Did she still have the card? She would look for it in the morning.

Chapter 13

Woodstock, New York, November, 1867: Hoping to Leave the Country

There is nothing as sweet as a comeback, when you are down and out, about to lose, and out of time.
Anne Lamott

To: Mr. Juan Manuel Macías
c/o Sociedad Republicana de Cuba y Puerto Rico
New York, New York

*D*ear Mr. Macías:

I was referred to you by our mutual friend Felix Grillo, who spoke highly of your intellect, integrity, and unswerving dedication to the cause of Cuba's independence. I am a Cuban myself and share your love for our beautiful land, and would like to contribute my talents in support of your goals.

I currently reside in upstate New York, but plan to return to the City as soon as possible. I, however, lack employment and am devoid of financial resources. Would your organization be able to assist me to get back on my feet upon my arrival in New York? I am a good writer (a poetess by trade) and a hard worker. Being a member of the weaker sex, I cannot promise I will take up arms to defend Cuba's freedom but intend to return eventually to my home in the Oriente province and work ceaselessly to liberate our blessed land.

Please let me know if you will be able to help me. If I receive positive news from you, I may be able to arrange for coming back to New York in a matter of weeks, before the worst of the winter weather sets in.

Hoping for favorable news from you, I remain your faithful servant

Miss Graciela Serrano

Chapter 14

Pilón, January, 1868: Walking the Tightrope

*I finally know what distinguishes man
from other beasts: financial worries.*
Jules Renard

For a change, Rocha's report was not gloomy. "The zafra is going well so far. No major equipment breakdowns or transportation delays. The Chinese workers are proving to be industrious and don't create problems the way slaves do. If the good luck continues, we may make it to the end of the season without too much trouble."

Ceclia was not enthusiastic. "We better do well. I had to empty our bank account to pay for all the things that had to be fixed last year."

Rocha had a suggestion: "I know you don't want to hear this, but if we run into any major trouble you may need to get a bank loan using the mill as collateral."

"Mortgaging our business? Leonardo would turn in his grave if we were to do such a thing!"

"I hope it never comes to pass, but if there is ever a need I have contacts with a lender in Santiago that might be able to give us a loan at a reasonable interest rate."

"Heaven forbid!" repeated Cecilia.

***

Finances were not Cecilia's only concern. She was increasingly upset about Carmela's infatuation with Yoyi, the guard. Cecilia disapproved of her daughter's distancing from Rodolfo, a man who was loving to his children and faithful to the family. On top of that, her daughter was taking up with an illiterate, lower class foreigner. This was immoral and reprehensible, and the fact that she made no effort to be discrete about the affair was shameful. "Rocha, the other guards, and probably half of the mill's workers know about it. It won't be long before the word spreads all over town. You will be branded as a puta."

"I don't care!" replied Carmela mulishly. "It's my life, and I'll lead it any way I want, thank you very much!"

"What do you see in this fellow, anyway? He is uncouth, ignorant, has terrible manners, and is incapable of holding a two-minute conversation about anything!"

"If you must know, our sex is wonderful, and he is nice to me and my children. I don't need to love a man to enjoy his company."

"The children! What kind of example are you setting for them? And how about Rodolfo? Don't you have any regard for your husband?"

"Rodolfo knows. I've told him."

"You have? And how has he reacted?"

"Like the fool he is! He does not like it, but he says that as long as the children do not suffer, he is willing to wait it out until I get back to my senses."

"He is a saint and you are a whore! I'm ashamed of having you as a daughter!"

"And I would pack up and go away from here if I only could, the way Graciela did."

At the mention of her lost older daughter, Cecilia could not hold back her tears. "I wish it was you the one who ran away rather than she!"

"Well, mother, maybe Yoyi will whisk me away to Santo Domingo."

"Don't you dare even say that! If you ran away leaving your children behind, I would never want to see your face again!"

Chapter 15

New York, December, 1867 - February, 1868: A Precipitous Return

People don't take trips, trips take people.
John Steinbeck

*I*n mid-December, Graciela received a brief response to her letter from Macías. The response read:

Estimada Srta. Serrano:

I am in receipt of your letter and am sorry for what I perceive to be your strained circumstances. It is the duty of the organization I have the honor of heading to assist our fellow nationals in every way we can, within the bounds of our limited means. I am enclosing the business card of a boarding house that can provide you with modest but comfortable accommodations upon your arrival back in New York. We have prepaid for up to seven days of your stay there, at the end of which you will have hopefully been able to make other arrangements. I regret our organization can not offer you paid employment, but your assistance as a volunteer would be most gratefully received.

I look forward to making your acquaintance soon, but suggest you delay your trip back to New York until fine weather returns. In the meantime, I remain,

Very truly yours,
Juan Manuel Macías
President, Sociedad Republicana de Cuba y Puerto Rico

***

Graciela intended to follow Macías' advice and delay taking any action on her personal situation until the spring. Events, however, prompted her return to New York in the middle of an unusually frigid winter. As the holidays passed and the worst of the cold set in, Evelyn started spending less time at home and took to going with Susie on trips that took the women as far east as Connecticut, or west to the Hunter West Kill Wilderness. Graciela felt increasingly abandoned and vulnerable, a young woman living alone in the woods, unprotected and risking all sorts of misadventures.

It was one Monday evening at the end of January that the situation became a crisis. Graciela had suffered a minor accident while cooking that left her right hand burned from hot grease, a wound that she had to take care of unaided and while in considerable pain. She had confronted Evelyn with what she perceived to be the consequences of her abandonment:

"You spend days and days out, gallivanting with your friend, leaving me alone and exposed. I could be attacked, or have a seizure or an accident like this, and there would be nobody around to help me. I'm tired of this!"

"What would you have me do?" replied Evelyn acidly. "You

are not a baby, and if you can't take care of yourself, that's your tough luck. If you don't like it here, you are free to take off! Nobody is keeping you here in shackles!"

In retrospect, Graciela should have kept her peace and waited for a more propitious time to call it quits, but she was in pain and angry and felt very tired of her life in this remote village, so she screamed back: "I want to get out of here!! You and Susie can have each other, and keep this shack, and stay in this dump of a town, but I want to go away!"

"Fine" replied Evelyn icily. "I'll get a carriage to take you back to New York! Start packing, because I want you out before the week is out!"

Chapter 16

La Habana, February, 1868: Caught

The practice of arbitrary imprisonments has been, in all ages,
the favorite and most formidable instruments of tyranny.
Alexander Hamilton

*T*he conspirators met in an old home in Revillagigedo Street, a few steps from the Church of Jesús María. The neighborhood, whose inhabitants were for the most part freed slaves, indigents, and other derelicts, was a slum that had grown over many decades outside the now torn down city wall, and it had always been regarded as one of the most disreputable sections of La Habana. Since it was also far from the University and the more affluent sections of the city, it was regarded as a safe, inconspicuous place in which to plan a revolt against the Spanish rule.

That night Carlos was away from the city and Irene refused to meet with what she called little kids playing at war, so Alberto and four other independentists were the only ones present at the meeting. They were discussing how to arrange for the distribution of subversive pamphlets that were being printed in secret by a shop in the new suburb of Marianao when there was a very loud knock on the door, followed by a shout from outside: "Police! Open up!"

Alberto looked around for a way to escape, but the house lacked a back door. He was sprinting towards the upstairs rooms thinking of perhaps jumping out of a window when there was a crash and the front door caved in from someone's brutal kick. Four uniformed men carrying pistols and shotguns barged into the room and pointed the weapons at its occupants menacingly. "You are all under arrest!" shouted the leader, a burly, mustachioed man sporting a black boina hat displaying a large yellow and red cockade as an emblem of rank.

"We've done nothing" protested one of Alberto's companions. The officer struck him on the side of the head with his shotgun, dropping him to the floor. "Cabrones, you are seditious cowards conspiring against the motherland!" replied the leader. "Anyone else want to say anything?" Alberto and his friends remained silent and were led away.

Chapter 17

New York, February, 1868: A Pleasant Surprise

Rags to riches isn't a story anyone wants to hear until after it's done.
Maggie Stiefvater

𝒯he boardinghouse that Macías had booked was barely adequate, but after a hair-raising ride through snow and ice Graciela was beyond exhausted and barely had enough strength to remove her clothes and fall into a dreamless sleep.

She woke up many hours later, feeling groggy and disoriented. After a cup of coffee in the common room, her mind cleared a bit and she began to re-examine her situation. She was back to where she started. Alone in a foreign land, with no money to her name, the funds she was counting on having largely disappeared on account of the stupid civil war that had raged in this country. Thinking of her essentially worthless trust account, she resolved she would pay a visit to Mr. Davis to see if there was any way to sell some of her holdings to secure some cash.

She dressed carefully, intending to make a good impression on the old man in whose hands her future might hinge. On her carriage ride to the Wall Street area, she started to ponder what she would do if no money could be made available to her. She was grimacing as she entered the vestibule of the Continental Trust Company's offices, expecting another pugnacious round with the receptionist that had almost denied her entrance the last time around. The same woman was at the counter; however, instead of a challenge Graciela was met with a surprised, if pleasant, smile. "Oh, Miss Serrano, I'm so glad to see you! Did you finally see our ads?"

"What ads?" replied Graciela, confused.

"Why, the several ads I myself placed in the "Personals" sections of the Times and the Daily News asking for you to contact this office."

"I am sorry, I have been out of town and have not read the local papers. What were these ads about?"

"One moment, please. Let me get Mr. Davis. He'll explain it all to you."

***

Theophilus Davis was all smiles as he led Graciela to an ostentatious conference room with plump chairs circling a mahogany table, soothing green wallpaper and prints of hunting scenes set in fancy gilded frames. "My dear Miss Serrano, I am so glad, indeed relieved, to see you again! Can I offer you some tea, or perhaps a cup of freshly brewed coffee?"

"No, thanks" replied Graciela, somewhat in shock. "What is the story with the newspaper ads that your assistant mentioned?"

"Oh, those!" Davis replied. "When your mother sent the funds, she instructed us to attempt by all means to disburse them to you as soon as possible, and since we did not have your address, we resorted to placing ads asking you to contact this office at your earliest convenience."

"Did Mother send me money?"

"She certainly did. She deposited two thousand dollars with us last September to be disbursed to you."

"Two thousand dollars!" exclaimed Graciela, in shock. "Do you mean to tell me that you can give me two thousand dollars in cash right now?"

"Well, two thousand minus transaction charges and expenses. I think the available net is about nineteen hundred and fifty-eight dollars and change."

"And those are mine for the asking?"

"Certainly. But may I suggest you make a partial withdrawal now and leave the bulk in your account with us? It is not safe for a single, young woman to be out on the street with such a large amount in her possession."

Graciela did a quick calculation. "How about if I withdraw one hundred dollars and keep the rest in your safe hands?"

"Wise idea" replied Mr. Davis.

"Can I have them now?"

"Certainly."

Chapter 18

Pilón, March, 1868: An Unexpected Visitor

So, beware of strangers.
Snow White and the Seven Dwarfs (1937)

*C*ecilia and Carmela watched apprehensively as the dusty and sweaty Black man dismounted from his panting horse and walked unsteadily towards the front door of the manor house. Visits from strangers on horseback usually signified bad news, and they already had their share of worries as the zafra had slowed down due to the sudden mass departure of Haitian workers, lured away by better paying offers of employment building new railway lines in the eastern part of the province.

The visitor wore the dark smock-frock and wide brimmed hat of a railroad worker and was carrying a large sheet of paper in his hand. Stopping before the women, he asked haltingly: "Is this the Serrano household?"

"Yes, it is" replied Cecilia. "What do you need?"

"I have been instructed to deliver to you this telegram that came to the Manzanillo railway office." He handed the paper to Cecilia, who read the following:

TO MANZANILLO RAILWAY MANAGER [STOP] DELIVER THIS MESSAGE TO HEAD OF SERRANO FAMILY PILON ORIENTE [STOP] YOUR SON ALBERTO LAZARO SERRANO IN CUSTODY CHARGED WITH SUBVERSIVE ACTIVITIES AGAINST THE

CROWN [STOP] BEING HELD PENDING TRIAL FOR SEDITION [STOP] MAY BE RELEASED UPON BAIL PAYMENT OF ONE THOUSAND SILVER ESCUDOS AND PERSONAL APPEARANCE BY FAMILY MEMBER AT GOVERNORS PALACE [STOP] ABSENT BAIL POSTING DEFENDANT WILL FACE TRIAL IN MAY AND POSSIBLE SENTENCE TO DEATH OR IMPRISONMENT [STOP] BY ORDER OF FRANCISCO LERSUNDI CAPITAN GENERAL [END]

Cecilia read the message twice and started to tremble. What was the meaning of this? Alberto had been in Spain with a Cuban delegation that sought political reforms, but was not a revolutionary, not a hothead. Her confusion was interrupted by the messenger, who asked timidly: "My boss asked that you confirm that you have received this message and understand it."

Cecilia managed to respond "Yes, I have" before breaking into tears.

***

Ceclia, Carmela and Rodolfo held a grim family meeting to decide what to do to rescue Alberto. Rodolfo once again volunteered: "I will go to La Habana again to get my brother-in-law out of jail." Cecilia shook her head in negation. "No, you have sacrificed once already. Besides, they may not accept you to be the one posting the bond."

"Nonsense" replied Rodolfo. "These jackals just want to extract money, don't care who delivers it."

Cecilia was unmoved. "We can't take any chances. I'm Alberto's mother, they can't deny my right to rescue my only son!"

"Alright, go" replied Carmela. "But who is going to run the mill in your absence?"

"Not you" shot back Cecilia acidly. "You have shown us lately that you have absolutely no common sense."

"What do we do, then?" insisted Carmela. "You know I don't trust Rocha, and don't like the way he looks at me. And our business should not be put in the hands of strangers."

"No need to. Rodolfo, can I put you in charge of managing the mill while I am gone?"

Rodolfo was dubious: "I've never run a business of any kind before, let alone a large operation."

"But you have a good head and are honest and trustworthy. Just don't make any major decisions if you can avoid them. I'll tell Rocha that he can run the day-to-day operations, but he must get your approval for anything major" insisted Cecilia.

"Mother, I'll do it if you ask me, but it's a heavy burden."

"I know, but I don't know where else to turn. Thank you for doing this for us."

Carmela had another objection: "I thought our bank account was empty. Where are we going to get a thousand silver escudos, plus the costs of travel for you and Alberto, because I assume you will be bringing him home with you."

"I'll get a loan. Rocha knows someone who can lend us money."

Chapter 19

New York, March - May, 1868: Decisions

The sun at home warms better than the sun elsewhere.
Albanian Proverb

*I*t **was a** chilly but sunny early spring afternoon. Graciela, out to retrieve some more funds from Mr. Davis, decided to have lunch out and took a short walk from Pine Street to Fraunces Tavern, the oldest restaurant in the city. Over chicken pot pie and tea, she sat in a remote corner of the always busy restaurant and examined her options.

It had been over a month since her return to New York and all she had accomplished was to spend money and wear out her boots in search of an acceptable job. It was not that work was unavailable; in such a big city, employment opportunities were plentiful – for maids, charwomen, waitresses, prostitutes. Graciela's problem was that she was unwilling to take a poor immigrant job but, although an educated woman, she lacked the specific training that would have qualified her to become a secretary or a nurse or even a teacher. She was a passable potter, but lacked the funds to open her own studio or rent space with other artists; a poet, but her rhymes were in Spanish and of no interest to the natives of this country.

The sad truth dawned on her: she had been trained to be a sophisticated, affluent lady of leisure in another country, a land she had left in a fit of pique over societal rejection of her sexuality. Coming to America she had gained personal freedom, but, no longer being wealthy, she had given up everything else. She fitted as poorly here as she had in Pilón; but at least at home she was not lacking in material comforts and was tolerated, if not necessarily loved, by her family. Was it time to go back? She resisted the idea, for going home would represent an admission of her folly, a loss of face she was loath to accept.

She consulted with Macías, whom she visited frequently to help with his organization's revolutionary activities. She went into the full details of the reasons for her leaving Cuba and contrasted her chagrin about her circumstances in the island with the inadequacy of her current situation in the States. After listening to her less than coherent ramble, Macías counseled:

"Dear Graciela, I love to have you here to continue helping liberate Cuba. From that standpoint, I would be tempted to recommend that you try to weather your current predicament and give yourself and New York a little more time. On the other hand, I suspect that you would be able to make a greater contribution to Cuba's independence back there than here."

Graciela had an idea: "Why don't I go back to Cuba, but stay in La Habana instead of returning to Pilón? The lifestyle in the big city might be more agreeable to me than the rigid country life I escaped a year ago."

Macías was not supportive: "Living in La Habana these days could be perilous for a person like you. As you are aware, since the possibility arose of the United States attempting to seize Cuba, the Spanish government has implemented a policy of fostering the emigration of its nationals into the island, in an effort to "rehispanize" Cuba with individuals loyal to the mother country. Those immigrants, now many thousands in number, have settled mainly in La Habana. They are young, uneducated, rough males who have turned into a paramilitary force bent on opposing those in the local population seen as potentially seditious. These men are known as voluntarios and will do harm to anyone considered to be liberal or non-conforming with traditional conservative Catholic norms. In La Habana, your political and personal preferences would make you a target, not only of the colonial government, but of the voluntarios as well. So, if you are going to return to Cuba, I recommend that you go to the eastern part of the country and stay clear of La Habana."

Graciela thanked the man for his counsel and declared: "I need to think about it, but thanks."

Two months later, Graciela was still unemployed and, as the funds in her bank account continued to dwindle, she booked passage on a steamer that would take her back to Santiago de Cuba.

Chapter 20

La Habana, April, 1868: Rescue

Pain is part of the price of freedom.
Daniel Kish

*C*ecilia hadn't been back to La Habana in the many years since the family had left and, under better circumstances, would have spent a bit of time taking in its many sights. As it was, the moment she was let off the boat that brought her to the city she seized her suitcase and hired a carriage to take it to the Plaza de Armas, which fortunately was not too far from the docks. On arrival, she paid scant attention to the impressive Baroque-styled palace, and proceeded across the central courtyard, where a marble monument to Christopher Columbus had recently been erected. On the left wing of the building was a stone staircase that led to the prison below, and Cecilia rushed down the steps dragging her suitcase, not caring to hide her anxiety.

The prison contained a gallery of windowless cells with heavy iron-barred doors whose occupants were monitored by the guards by standing before the door and peering inside through small barred windows. The only illumination available in each cell was provided by metal candelabra holding tallow candles. The stench emanating from the cells was overpowering and Cecilia could sense it the moment she reached the last steps in the stairway.

Outside the cell complex was a guard room, which at the time of Cecilia's late afternoon arrival was occupied by a single officer, a rubicund, heavy-set man in full uniform and boina hat. He looked at Cecilia with evident distaste and greeted her rudely in a voice that betrayed a heavy Northern Spain accent: "What do you want, lady? This is no place for women."

"My name is Cecilia Marín de Serrano and am here to bail out my son Alberto" replied Cecilia.

"Oh, Albertico! The whiny little brat!" went on the guard in an insulting tone.

"Sir, he is my son, and I have come to get him out of here!" Cecilia bellowed.

"Do you have the bail?"

"I have a bank note for one thousand silver escudos, as requested."

The guard opened a large book and thumbed through the pages. "The bail is one thousand and twenty escudos, lady."

Cecilia blanched and nervously went through her purse and extracted the fatal telegram. "Here, this is from Captain General Lersundi, setting the bail as one thousand escudos."

"And I say it is one thousand and twenty. You can give me the bank note and twenty escudos in coin."

"That is preposterous!" screamed Cecilia. "I will do no such a thing!"

"Well, you can take it up with Captain Escalante when he comes back tomorrow, but he will tell you the same thing. So, either pay up now or get out of here."

Cecilia realized she was being blackmailed and would have to pay the guard a bribe to get Alberto released. She dug deeply into her purse, rummaged through its contents, and started counting coins. "All I have is sixteen escudos" she lamented, producing eight large coins. "I guess I'll have to come back tomorrow and talk to your captain."

"I tell you what. It's time for me to go home. I'll take the bank note and the sixteen escudos. Anything to get rid of that cur." He produced two copies of a written form, which he filled out with the details of the release. "Here is one receipt for you and one for us. Please sign each form on the bottom left, and I'll sign on the right. Note that your son is released on his promise that he will voluntarily appear when his case is heard by the court at a later date."

Cecilia grimaced but signed both forms and handed them back to the guard. He got up and retrieved a large bundle of keys from a nook on the wall. "Wait here" he admonished.

He returned a few moments later, dragging a stumbling young man who freed himself from the guard's grip and lurched to Cecilia's arms. "Mother!" he cried hoarsely. Cecilia embraced him tightly and replied, keeping her tears in check: "Let's get out of here!"

***

Cecilia had to help Alberto up the steps with one hand and carry her suitcase with the other, and they moved clumsily towards the front entrance of the palace, where she waved at the line of cabs that waited for fares outside the building. "Where are we going?" asked Alberto haltingly.

"I have booked a room at a hotel in this area" started Cecilia, turning to the driver to give him directions.

"No, let's go to my room first. I want to see Irene!"

"Who is Irene?"

"She is my girlfriend, soon to be my wife!"

"You never told me you had a girlfriend!"

"I was planning on bringing her home to meet you" replied Alberto sheepishly.

"There is a lot you haven't told me," grumbled Cecilia, and then caught herself. "But there is time for all the talking. Tell the driver where we want to go."

Chapter 21

Pilón, April, 1868: A Breakup

*Never allow someone to be your priority while
allowing yourself to be their option.*
Mark Twain

*C*armela took the opportunity to move Yoyi into her bedroom when Cecilia went to La Habana. At first, their life together was an unending stream of exciting couplings, tender caresses, and sweet words, with each party reveling in the other's admiration. Their idyll was only interrupted by the demands of Yoyi's duties as a guard at the mill, which he discharged with increasing distaste. Carmela started to wonder how to convince her mother to hire Yoyi directly and give him a trivial job that would not interfere with her sex life, a proposition Cecilia would likely resist.

Meanwhile, Rodolfo kept to the visitors' guesthouse and only came to the manor in the afternoons after work, to visit with the children and take them out to play or in short excursions around town. He kept his jealousy at his adulterous wife's activities to himself, but other drinking patrons at *El Malecón* became aware of his morose mood and gave him a wide berth.

Then came that Wednesday night. Carmela and Yoyi had gone to bed late after a heavy meal in which a lot of Rioja had been consumed and had fallen asleep next to each other, too sat-

212

ed to even kiss. Hours later, when the first light of dawn began filtering through the bedroom's French window shutters, Yoyi woke up with a start. He cursed: he was soon due to relieve Luc, who had the night duty that week. He began waking up and realized he had an erection and felt a sudden urge that needed satisfying.

He elbowed Carmela and, when she did not respond, shook her vigorously. "Come on, Carmela, wake up!" he prompted.

"Leave me alone!" she muttered, still caught in some dream that refused to be dismissed.

"Come on, darling, I have this itch that I need you to satisfy!"

"Itch?" answered Carmela, turning her body away from his. "Scratch yourself!"

Yoyi shook her roughly and replied in a louder voice: "Come on, you are my wench and I need satisfaction!"

At the word "wench," Carmela became instantly awake. She had a terrible headache and had not slept enough, and was in no mood to be bothered. "What do you mean I am your wench?" she challenged.

Had he been more awake and in control of himself, Yoyi would perhaps have smoothed over the situation with some self-deprecating remark. But he was half drunk, horny, and in a hurry, so he shook her again and replied: "Yes, you are my hussy, you floozy, and it's time you open your legs because I have need of your services."

Carmela sat up in a jerk, pushing Yoyi's arm vigorously away. "So that's what I am to you? A container for your jism?"

Again, Yoyi could have defused the situation by apologizing profusely. Instead, he got up and put on his pants. "Aw, forget it! I have no time for your bitching. I'll talk to you tonight!" he shouted and barged out.

Carmela, now alone and wide awake, reflected on the course of her romance with Yoyi. Her only other affair had been with her husband, and Rodolfo had always been loving and tender, if perhaps a bit dull. He had always treated her as royalty, and if there had been faults in his behavior, lack of respect was not one.

She had clearly mistaken physical attraction for affection. But she was not a whore; she could do without the likes of Yoyi and link up, if it came to pass, with a higher quality person. She would go to Rocha and ask that Yoyi be fired or reassigned by the contractor to another job away from Pilón.

Chapter 22

La Habana, April, 1868: News

A grand adventure is about to begin.
Winnie the Pooh

On the ride over to Alberto's room, Cecilia was able to take a good look at her son and was appalled. Alberto had lost a lot of weight and exhibited ugly bruises on the face and arms; probably he had others under his clothes, which were filthy rags that stank to high heaven. "What did they do to you?" she asked, alarmed.

"Never mind that" replied Alberto, taking a deep sigh. "It's all over now." After a silent moment, he continued: "But they will pay!"

When they arrived, Cecilia realized she had only some loose change left in her purse. "I'll go to the Banco del Comercio tomorrow to draw some funds. I hope your girlfriend is home and has money for the driver."

"I'll check" replied Alberto, limping out of the carriage.

Moments later he returned, accompanied by a striking redhead who did not look like anyone Cecilia had ever met. The young woman approached the driver and paid him, and then walked over to the passenger bench and helped Cecilia dismount.

"I'm Irene, and am SOOO happy to meet you!"

The girl embraced Cecilia, took charge of her suitcase, and

led the way upstairs to the room she shared with Alberto.

***

"Go take a bath and throw those clothes in the trash!" demanded Irene. "I'll talk to your mother in the meantime."

Cecilia's first reaction to the assertive young woman was one of confusion. She had been raised in a culture in which women were subservient to the males in their lives and had to achieve their goals through patience and cunning. This flaming hair girl did not seem disposed to bend to the will of others, including her men. But, as they began their conversation, she realized there was kindness and love beneath Irene's brashness.

"How did you meet my son?" inquired Cecilia.

"He took a heavy blow to the head to protect me during a demonstration last year. I figured I owed him one after that" replied Irene airily.

"It was the shoulder!" objected Alberto, emerging from the washroom. He had fresh trousers on but was naked from the waist up.

"Oh, my God!" exclaimed Cecilia, looking at the collection of bruises of all hues that covered her son's upper body.

"Did they torture you?" asked Irene.

"Yes, but I gave them nothing. But they knew most of it anyhow. Ramiro was a spy, a Spanish informer that betrayed us and gave the police chapter and verse on our group."

"Is your friend Carlos part of your group?" asked Cecilia.

"Yes, but they didn't get him. I suppose he is hiding somewhere."

"We need to take you home and hide you from these animals in case they want to go ahead with taking you to court" warned Cecilia.

"I think those are probably terror tactics" commented Irene. "But I agree that you will be safer back home, than you are here."

"I already lost one child to the United States. I want Alberto home with me for the time being" replied Cecilia.

"And I want Irene to travel back with us" announced Alberto.

"What makes you think I would want to go with you?" started Irene mockingly. But then she added: "But given my condition, I guess I should do any travel now rather than later."

"What do you mean condition?" snapped Alberto.

"I'm almost three months pregnant" announced Irene. "You will be a father by Christmas."

Chapter 23

Pilón, June, 1868: Comings and Goings

There is a time for departure even when there's no certain place to go.
Tennessee Williams

Cecilia, **Alberto and Irene** arrived in Pilón after a boat and carriage ride that had taken an unusually long time because of rough weather. Irene, who had never traveled by sea, experienced continuous bouts of dizziness, nausea, and vomiting, her seasickness made worse by her pregnancy, and was irritable and argumentative. Mother and son suffered the girl's bad mood as well as they could, and spent much of the time comforting her and each other and wondering what the future held in store for them.

The moment they came through the door, Yaya rushed in and clung to his master in a tight, tear-stained embrace, and then quickly went over to the brass calling card table by the front door, retrieved a parchment envelope and handed it to Alberto: "This was delivered by hand a couple of days ago. It's important!"

Cecilia chided the slave: "Yaya! Did you open that envelope?"

"Miss Cecilia, the messenger who brought it said it was urgent!"

Alberto extracted a folded note from the envelope and read aloud:

Alberto, come join me at my uncle's farm as soon as possible. You are not safe at home! I am told L. is going to start picking up all known and suspected infidentes and jail or deport them. You are likely to be arrested in a few days if you stay at home. We will shelter you.

C.

(Please destroy this note after reading it.)

Everyone in the room started talking at once. Cecilia, who had turned white as a ghost, asked feebly: "Who is L?" Alberto and Irene responded in unison: "Lersundi, the bastard that is now Captain General."

"Is the threat mentioned by Carlos real?" asked Cecilia tremulously.

"You know Carlos. He is a serious fellow. He may be wrong, but he put himself at risk by sending me this letter" replied Alberto.

"At least we know he is safe" commented Irene.

"I probably should leave right away for Manzanillo" continued Alberto.

"I'll go with you!" responded Irene.

"You should stay here" replied Alberto. "Nobody is looking for you and Carlos and his family are well-known opponents of the Spanish rule. I may be running into trouble by going there, but there is no reason for you and my son to be placed at risk also."

"Your son?" started Irene, sarcastically. "Aren't you anticipating things a little?"

Cecilia cut in. "Nobody is going anywhere, at least not today. Let's rest for a day or two and recover from the trip from La Habana before taking off again. I will start making arrangements for someone to take Alberto to Manzanillo discretely. Let's unpack and …" She could not go on because of the tears.

***

Three days later, just before dawn, Alberto took off for Manzanillo in a closed carriage, witnessed by four women and a man giving signs of grief; even Yaya, the old Black slave, was part of the melancholic tableau that saw him off. The man, Rodolfo, embraced his old friend and vowed to look after the family for as long as he was gone. "But come back as soon as you can, you hear?" were his parting words.

Alberto had been gone less than two weeks when, one afternoon, half a dozen soldiers arrived at the manor house, banging at the front door and demanding entrance. Yaya opened the door and the leader of the group shoved her aside, commanding: "Get your mistress, now!" When a pale Cecilia came into the living room the soldier asked peremptorily: "I have an order for the arrest of one Alberto Serrano, who is said to live in this house. Is he here?"

Cecilia, her face set into a rigid mask, replied: "No, Sir. He has gone to La Habana on business."

A voice from behind the group of soldiers commented: "She is lying, officer. Serrano has left town and is gone into hiding." It was Faustino Rocha.

***

The soldiers left after delivering a stiff warning to the family that aiding an *infidente* was a crime punishable by fines, a prison sentence, and confiscation of one's property. Rocha stayed behind, looking a bit contrite.

"How could you have betrayed us, Rocha?" demanded Cecilia.

"I had to make sure I was in the authorities' good graces, to protect my investment."

"What investment?" asked Carmela.

Rocha hesitated for a moment, and then replied: "When your mother needed money a couple of months ago, I helped her get a loan backed by a mortgage on the mill's assets from a lender in Santiago. A few days ago, I acquired the mortgage. So, I am your lender now and your assets are security for my loan. I have to make sure I am regarded as loyal to the Crown in case I need to foreclose on my loan and they try to seize the property."

"Foreclose? What are you talking about?" protested Cecilia.

"You know, your business is in trouble. The zafra is over now and the mill's production has been low and the sugar prices on the market are also lower, so you may not be able to continue paying the interest on your loan to me."

"And where did you get the money to buy the mortgage on our property?" challenged Cecilia.

"Señora, that is my own business."

Chapter 24

Santiago de Cuba, June, 1868: Cold Feet

Once I make up my mind, I'm full of indecision.
Oscar Levant

*G*raciela arrived in Santiago one hot afternoon after a long sea voyage, feeling apprehensive about her upcoming meeting with her mother. The additional trip to Pilón, 40 leagues away, would require a good couple of days ride and she could not muster the energy or drive to make transportation arrangements, so she decided to spend some time in town to recover and prepare herself for the ordeal that awaited. She got a room in a boardinghouse near the center of the city and did little but sleep and eat for the next two days.

As her energy was restored, a discarded idea re-emerged in modified form. La Habana might be too perilous for her, but how about getting a local job and spending a season in Santiago? The old city was ossified, remaining the same backwards village it had been for over three centuries. Except for hurricanes and earthquakes, nothing happened in Santiago, no voluntarios or Spanish troops terrorized the population. As long as her behavior was discrete, she would remain ignored.

It seemed like a good plan, one that would allow her to postpone the confrontation with her family. It suffered, however, from the same flaw that had forced her out of the United States: she could not get gainful employment, and the job market in Santiago was much smaller than it had been in New York. She visited the local government offices inquiring about teaching, nursing, secretarial and other clerical positions. The city, like the rest of the island, was in the midst of an economic downturn due a crisis in the sugar industry caused by fluctuations in the global market and rising production costs; few new positions were available and she was judged insufficiently qualified to fill them.

Two weeks into her fruitless job search she was in the middle of one of her interviews, this time at the main post office, when the Spaniard who served as postmaster asked her: "And where are you from? You sound like you are from this area."

"Not far from here" replied Graciela. "I'm from Pilón, west of here near Cabo Cruz."

"Pilón, eh? One of my runners goes that way and says Pilón is beautiful, on the coast so close to Cabo Cruz."

Graciela felt a sudden pang of nostalgia. "My family owns a sugar mill in Pilón."

"I hear most sugar mills are in trouble these days. I hope your family's is still doing well."

Graciela excused herself the best she could and went back to the boardinghouse to pack and find a carriage ride. Her procrastination was over. It was time to check on her family.

Chapter 25

Pilón, June, 1868: Discovery

Even a blind squirrel finds an acorn now and again.
Will Smith

*I*t was merienda time, and Rodolfo had come over as usual to take the children out for their midafternoon break. Cecilia met him at the front door, led him to the drawing room, and sat next to him. "Listen, Rodolfo, we have a problem. Rocha is pressuring me to dismiss you; I don't think he wants you around to check on him. Is there anything you can do to find out more about what he has been up to since he came onboard? I would fire him but I can't, since he is our landlord now, but I need some ammunition to confront him in case he tries to pull something on us."

Rodolfo took Cecilia's hand reassuringly. "I can try to do some digging after work tonight."

Later that night, Cecilia, Irene and Carmela sat in the dining room after supper playing brisca when Rodolfo knocked insistently on the front door. Yaya let him in and he entered quickly and joined the ladies. Cecilia greeted him: "Oh, Rodolfo, what are you doing here this late? Come, sit with us."

Rodolfo remained standing. His body rocked and he clenched his fists as if was struggling to contain his anger. He spoke with great agitation: "I found it! The bastard has been stealing from us for years!!"

Cecilia got up, took Rodolfo gently by the arm, and sat him across from Carmela. "What did you find?"

Rodolfo strained to calm down enough to speak. "Do you know the mahogany bureau that Leonardo had in the mill office?"

"Yes. I got it for him as a present when we bought the mill back in '56."

"Well, the lower drawer on the right has a false bottom that I never knew existed until tonight. I was familiar with the contents of the bureau, but began taking papers out and going through them without finding anything of interest until I accidentally tapped the bottom of the lower drawer and noticed it sounded hollow. I took a knife and lifted the bottom of the drawer up and discovered a hidden stack of papers that included receipts and correspondence between Rocha and various vendors, such as the New Orleans shop that did the steam engine overhaul years ago and several other jobs. Each invoice shows the amount charged to the mill and the rebate to be paid to Rocha, usually fifty percent. In three years, he has racked up many thousands of escudos in kickbacks from vendors, repair shops, and suppliers."

"I knew he could not be trusted!" commented Carmela. "But he managed to charm Mother with all his piropos and sweet words!"

"I'm sorry if I fell for it" replied Cecilia bitterly. "An old woman like me can use a kind phrase every once in a while."

"What are we going to do?" wondered Carmela.

"I should have retrieved those papers" lamented Rodolfo, "but I was in a rush to tell you what I found out, so I closed the secret compartment and left things as they were before leaving. I'll go back to the mill now, grab them, and bring them to you."

Cecilia gave Rodolfo some quick orders: "We'll hire a lawyer and let him tell us what to do. There is this guy in Niquero who used to do stuff for us over the years. I'll go see him tomorrow. Now, get the papers quickly and bring them here. I will put them in a safe place."

Chapter 26

Pilón, June, 1868: Moments too Late

One doesn't recognize the really important moments in one's life until it's too late.
Agatha Christie

The cover of the secret compartment of the lower drawer of the bureau had come up easily last time Rodolfo had pried at its edge with a knife. This time around, however, the cover, perhaps misplaced, resisted Rodolfo's attempts at lifting it and he did not dare apply too much force to it lest he break the thin slat of wood. He was so intent on his struggle with the drawer that he did not hear the approaching steps. Moments later, the light of a kerosene lamp, held high by Yoyi, shone on the scene.

Startled, Rodolfo attempted to get up but Luc, who stood next to Yoyi, pushed him down brutally. "You waits here!" growled the guard.

Moments later Lester and Rocha barged into the office. Rocha challenged Rodolfo: "What were you doing here in the middle of the night messing with my papers?"

Rodolfo faced his accuser with uncontrolled rage: "I know what you have been doing, Faustino. Cheating these poor women out of their last penny! Shame on you!"

Rocha motioned Luc to pull Rodolfo up from the chair and replied diffidently: "La ocasión hace al ladrón." Then he questioned: "What did you see?"

"Everything! All your dirty deals! But you will pay for it, I swear!"

Rocha smirked: "I don't think you will be the one to make me pay." Then he directed the guards: "Let's get him out of here and into the woods."

Luc forced Rodolfo to get on his feet and led him towards the office's door. As they approached the exit, Rodolfo turned around suddenly, punched Luc in the face, wrestled the shotgun out of his captor's hand, and pointed the weapon at Rocha. "You won't get me so easily, bastards!"

Before he could make good on his threat, however, the others reacted. Yoyi and Lester fired their weapons simultaneously, striking Rodolfo at point blank on his chest and abdomen. Rodolfo keeled over and fell to the floor.

"Finish him off" ordered Rocha.

"With pleasure" replied Yoyi, pointing his shotgun at Rodolfo's temple.

As Yoyi fired, Rocha lamented: "It's going to be a mess to get rid of the body. Let's drag him out of here!"

***

They discovered Rodolfo's body in the guesthouse where he lived. There were signs that the bullet-ridden corpse had been dragged into the guesthouse from elsewhere, and a blood trail ran out of the front door towards the mill's main building. None of the mill security guards could be found to be interrogated.

"I fired all of them two days ago" insisted Rocha. "They were missing work or showing up late, and were sloppy in their patrols." The mill was not in operation during the offseason, but one or two shop workers thought they had seen Luc the day of the crime. The Spanish authorities declined to investigate further on the grounds that Rodolfo had clearly been the victim of a robbery attempt.

"There is no justice for us" lamented Cecilia. "But, all the same, I will go to Niquero after the funeral to talk to my lawyer." Irene, always skeptical of Cuba's Spanish rulers, commented: "Go ahead, but it will be a waste of your time and money."

They were in the middle of the wake when a carriage arrived from Santiago bringing in a surprised Graciela, who joined in the lamentations after an emotional greeting from her mother and sister.

Carmela then left her grieving children in the custody of Cecilia, explaining: "I have to do something important." Ignoring Cecilia's questions, Carmela left the wake and rode over to the first aid cottage at the edge of town. She listened impatiently to the nuns' condolences and asked to speak to Carlos, the old black slave who, nine years before, had helped her elope with Rodolfo. Carlos expressed his grief over Rodolfo's passing but Carmela cut him short: "Do you remember *Los Suspiros*, the farm near Yara where you took me and Rodolfo after we got married?"

"Yes, señora, I do."

"And do you recall Rino, my husband's brother who got burned and shot my uncle and mother?"

"I sure do!"

"And do you still go to Manzanillo on errands for the nuns?"

"Yes, but not as often as I used to. I'm getting on years, you know."

"Well, I need you to do me a big favor."

From the questions, Carlos could already guess what the favor was. "Anything, ma'am. For you and master Rodolfo, may he rest in peace."

"I need you to go to Yara and see if you can locate Rino. He and a bunch of outlaws were operating on the mountains in the vicinity of *Los Suspiros*. If you find him, please let him know of my husband's death and deliver this urgent letter to him from me." She produced an envelope and handed it to Carlos. "I will understand it if you don't succeed in locating Rino, but in any case, would you please let me know how you did?"

She produced a little bag and proffered it to the slave. Carlos refused it energetically. "I don need no money. I'd be glad to run this errand for you and your husband."

"Thank you very much. I have to go back to Rodolfo's funeral, but please get in touch with me soon."

"Will do, ma'am. Give my sympathy to your mother."

Chapter 27

Pilón, June, 1868: A Somber Reunion

What epitaph, I wonder, would a poet write for him?
Euripides, The Trojan Women

Rodolfo's funeral was surprisingly well attended, due perhaps to his ability to make no enemies and win people over with his outgoing personality. One of the funeral attendees was Ernestina Cueto, who attempted to keep out of the sight of Graciela, who nevertheless sauntered in her direction and went directly to the point:

"Ernestina, thank you very much for coming. I am sure that Rodolfo would be grateful that you came to say your goodbyes to him, despite what happened between us."

Ernestina shrugged her shoulders. "I did not know him well, but he was a nice guy. And your mother was very nice to me when you went away."

"About my going away, I apologize. It was vain and arrogant of me to have left the way I did. But the good news is that I have learned an important lesson."

"What is that?"

"I don't give a damn anymore about what other people say. I am going to lead my life on my own terms, no matter what."

"I'm glad to hear that."
"Will you forgive me?"
"Maybe."
"Can we see each other again?"
"Maybe."
"Alright. Let's see what the time brings."
"Yes. Let's."

Chapter 28

Pilón, July, 1868: Justice and Sorrow

Injuries are revenged; crimes are avenged.
Samuel Johnson

*T*hree **weeks after** Rodolfo's funeral, another brutal crime stunned the erstwhile placid Pilón community. Faustino Rocha's corpse was discovered in his home; he had been beheaded, mutilated, and apparently tortured before being put to death. This time the authorities vowed to capture the sadistic criminal, but were unsuccessful.

In the months that followed, two of the former Santa Cruz security guards were found dead under mysterious circumstances. Since they were foreign nationals, their deaths passed unremarked and were not investigated.

After Rodolfo's funeral, the Serrano women and Irene set out to rebuild their lives. Rocha left no known survivors, and the mortgage he held – which had not been registered in the province's records – was never located. After a frantic search, Cecilia was able to find and hire a temporary manager to oversee the preparations for the mill's next zafra. She was still seeking a buyer for *Santa Cruz* but supervening events made the sale almost impossible.

Life continued but normality never resumed. Rodolfo's

death continued to weigh heavily on all, but most particularly on Carmela and her children. She mourned him and lamented daily his loss and her foolishness. She came to realize that Rodolfo had been the one, true love of her life, a gift from heaven she had squandered and would never be able to replace. She was finally achieving maturity, at a very high cost.

Epilogue

O**n October 10, 1868,** on his farm La Demajagua, near Yara, Carlos Manuel de Céspedes launched the armed insurrection against Spanish rule with the cry of "Viva Cuba libre!" He proclaimed the independence of Cuba and was joined by a hundred and fifty revolutionaries, including two young men: Alberto Serrano and Carlos Masó. In the manifesto that accompanied the call to arms, Céspedes explained: "Spain imposes on us an armed force on our territory which has no other goal than to submit us to the implacable yoke which degrades us." Céspedes ordered the release of all slaves, starting with his own, thus making the emancipation of all slaves the first political act of the newly proclaimed Cuban nation. He then invited all freed slaves, and all the people of Cuba, to join in a war of liberation: a war that was to last a full decade.

Alberto had met Céspedes in Manzanillo, on the farm of the Masó family, where Serrano was hiding from the Spanish army's pursuit. He soon discovered they shared an unforgettable memory: they both had witnessed the execution of Narciso López in 1851 and had been revolted by it. Céspedes had publicly protested the act and had been jailed on account of it; Alberto, a mere child, had vowed to himself he would some day do something about it. That day had arrived on the morning of October 10.

Alberto fought in the war until he fell in action in 1869 in the Battle of El Salado. He left behind a son he never met, Alberto Lázaro Serrano Cowan, and two nephews from his sister Carmela, Rodolfo and Lázaro Galán, all of whom would grow to be involved in the 1895 war that brought about Cuba's final independence from Spain. But that is a story for another day.

The Serrano women, then and always, continued to endure.